FOUND IN THE LOST
THE LEONIDAS CORPORATION
BOOK ONE

TARINA DEATON

Edited by
JESSICA SNYDER

TARINA DEATON LLC

For those who are still searching.

Not all who wander are lost.

CHAPTER 1

Kinley Dunn paced the length of the small arrivals hall of the Flores, Guatemala airport. Thirty-four steps one way, thirty-four steps the other way. She'd made the trip twelve times, checking her phone at the end of each round trip for any message from her mentor. Nothing. Dr. Banks wasn't answering any of her calls either.

She'd checked the date, her previous emails, the calendar invite, her tickets, her hotel reservation in Carmelita—everything she could think of to verify she was where she was supposed to be, when she was supposed to be.

Being invited on this dig was the chance of a lifetime, especially since she wasn't a field-trained archaeologist. This was her opportunity to show that it didn't matter if all of her experience was in the classroom. So what if she didn't have thousand-year-old dirt under her nails? She still had something to offer.

Stopping at the end of another round trip, she closed her eyes. "You were specifically invited on this trip because you did what no one else has been able to do. Your input into this discovery will be invaluable and change everything scholars thought they knew about Mayan culture and history. You are not a fraud."

She sighed after whispering her self-pep talk and glanced around, looking for any friendly face. Her gaze caught on the mop of blond curls and broad shoulders of a guy sitting in one of the many rows of chairs in the waiting area. Nice. But even a square jaw and five o'clock shadow couldn't distract her from the predicament of being stranded at an airport in Guatemala. No matter what she told herself, she couldn't *not* worry that someone had decided she shouldn't be there and just forgot to tell her because she was insignificant and not worth the time.

Slipping her arms from the straps of her large pack, she let it fall to the floor and stifled a groan. After a bend at the waist to stretch the abused muscles of her lower back, she settled the pack between her legs, half under the worn leather seat, and sat down at the end of an empty row. She had to bite the bullet. She had to call the other team lead. Taking a deep breath, she hit the dial button and exhaled slowly while it rang.

"Dr. Biert."

Kinley expelled the rest of her breath upon hearing his curt answer.

"Dr. Biert, this is Kinley Dunn. I'm sorry to bother you, but have you heard from Dr. Banks? She was supposed to meet me—"

"No. I haven't. Why are you calling me?"

Kinley bit back her initial curt response. "She was supposed to meet me at the Flores airport to take me to Carmelita, but she's not here."

"And?"

She looked down at the toes of her well-worn hiking boots and tapped her feet. "Do you know if there's someone else coming to meet me?"

"How the hell would I know that? Quit wasting my time with your petty issues and figure it out." With that, he ended the call.

Kinley pressed her lips together and mouthed, "Asshole." One of the most knowledgeable archaeologists in their field or not, he was still a grade A jerk.

Since he hadn't told her that she'd wasted her time and was no longer needed, she would have to figure out how to get herself to Carmelita now and figure out what happened to Dr. Banks later. She opened the web browser on her phone and searched for transportation from Flores to Carmelita.

"Damn it," she muttered. The last bus left twenty minutes ago.

"Excuse me."

Kinley looked up from her phone. A man leaned over the seat between them, smiling at her with his perfect white teeth. She hadn't even noticed him sit down. With his crisp, white button-down, black slacks and perfectly coifed hair, he looked out of place among the tourists and local travelers.

"I couldn't help but overhear your conversation," he said. "I am heading to Carmelita myself—I'm happy to offer you a ride." His English held a hint of an accent, the kind that should be sexy.

The tiny hairs on the back of her neck stood up. Nothing in his outward appearance screamed sinister serial killer, but something didn't feel right about the offer. Call it her sixth sense or female intuition, but whatever it was told her not to accept the offer.

"Thank you, but I'll figure it out," she said.

"It can be very tedious to get from Flores to Carmelita on the bus. I have a private car. I promise I am a perfect gentleman."

What was it the internet said? If a guy has to tell you he's a nice guy, he's not a nice guy? Every hair on her body was waving at her, shouting, "Stranger danger!"

"I'm meeting a group of friends at their hotel tonight," she lied. "I'll ride with them in the morning."

He shrugged and tilted his head. "As you wish. Good luck on your journey." He stood and slipped a hand in his pants pocket to pull out a pair of sunglasses, sliding them on his face as he walked toward the exit.

Where was his luggage? He didn't even have a briefcase or carry-on. Nothing to indicate he'd flown into the airport.

A shiver ran up her back, making her shoulders jump. She glanced toward the row of tour companies on the far side of the arrivals hall. Maybe there was a tour bus she could hop on.

Slinging her large hiking pack over one shoulder, she kept an eye on the path ahead of her and scrolled through the list of tour companies on her phone while she headed that direction. One company looked promising—they had private cars for smaller groups instead of buses. She paused and scanned the area, finding the small counter for the tour company toward the far corner.

Tucking her phone into the pocket of her cross-body travel purse, she strode with purpose right up until the moment her feet stopped moving and her upper body lurched forward.

The cracked and dusty tile rushed toward her and the heavy pack tumbled off her shoulder, throwing her even more off balance. She thrust out an arm to stop her fall and squeezed her eyes shut, bracing for impact.

A tight band encircled her waist and jerked her into a hard wall.

"Whoa there," a low, deep voice said in her ear.

Her heart fluttered as she realized the wall at her back was likely a warm chest belonging to the voice vibrating in her ear. The arm around her loosened and she inhaled deeply.

"You good?" the voice asked.

She nodded. "Yes."

The arm released her slowly, the fingers trailing across the bottom of her ribs to rest on her hip. "Hang on a sec."

Trying to ignore the goosebumps rolling across her skin, Kinley glanced down at the man now kneeling at her feet. He pressed a hand to the back of her knee and she lifted her foot while he untangled the black mesh strap of his bag from her ankle.

He stood and her eyes followed him up as he rose.

"Sorry about that," he said.

"That's...." She swallowed, and then shook her head. "It's my fault. I wasn't watching where I was going."

His lips spread in a slow smile she could only describe as mischievous and a little sexy. "So it's neither of our faults—just a lucky happenstance." He bent down, picked up her pack as if it weighed nothing, and held it out to her.

She wasn't sure almost biting the dust could be counted as lucky, but his catching her was, definitely. Taking her pack, she hefted it back onto her shoulder. "Yeah. Uh...thanks."

"Any time." He winked and resumed his seat.

It clicked that his shoulders were the ones she'd admired earlier. He was even better looking up close. His long lashes brushed his high cheek bones and were slightly darker than his blond hair, which was a little too long and curled around the tops of his ears. Could ears be cute?

Giving herself a mental shake, she made her way to the tour counter, watching where she stepped. *"Hola. ¿Habla usted inglés?"* she asked.

"Yes, I speak English." His nametag read Francisco.

"Thank goodness." She set her pack at her feet. "My Spanish is horrible. I need to get to Carmelita. Do you have any cars going that way I could ride with? I'm willing to pay for the transportation."

"We can only transport tour guests. You would have to pay for an entire tour."

Kinley's shoulders sagged. "Really? I only need a ride to Carmelita to meet with the rest of my group. The person who was supposed to meet me isn't here and the last bus of the day left. The rest of my group is leaving Carmelita in the morning and I really need to be there before then."

"I'm sorry, *señorita*," he said softly. "The policy is very strict."

Tired and on the verge of tears, she could only thank him for his time. She'd find a hotel for the night and take the first bus in the morning and figure out how to catch up with the group once she reached the office in Carmelita.

"She can ride with us."

Kinley's head whipped to the side. Her rescuer was rescuing her again.

"*Señor*, if she's not booked on the trip we can't act as a taxi for her."

"It's fine. I—"

"We originally booked four people, but one of our friends had to bail at the last minute. She's taking his spot." He raised his eyebrows and smiled. He leaned on the counter, causing his biceps to bulge and strain the fabric of his dark green T-shirt. With his curly blond hair and golden tan, he brought to mind the image of a surfer.

Kinley glanced at Francisco. He looked skeptical, to say the least.

"The cost of the tour is the same whether we have two people or twelve, so it doesn't matter if we add another person at the last minute." His tone was a little less friendly than before.

Francisco sighed and asked for her passport.

Euphoric relief surged through her. Trying not to grin like an idiot, she dug it out of her purse and handed it to him. Her rescuer tapped the counter and winked before returning to his seat and picking up his book.

"Miss?" Francisco returned her passport and gestured toward the sitting area. "Your car will depart when the rest of your group arrives."

"Thank you." Taking her bag over to the chairs, she sat one seat away from the man who had saved her ass, literally and figuratively, twice in the last few minutes. Why wasn't her female intuition freaking out about his offer? It wasn't even an offer or an ask. He demanded Francisco add her to their trip and she didn't even blink. Not only was her intuition not freaking out, her uterus was basically waving her fallopian tubes back and forth screaming, "Pick me! Pick me!"

"Thank you." She glanced at him through her eyelashes. "I wasn't looking forward to trying to find a hotel then coming back here tomorrow to catch the bus."

He placed a bookmark between the pages of his novel and shut it. "No problem. I guess it's fortuitous that my friends' flight was delayed. We were supposed to leave an hour ago."

His words echoed what he'd said earlier when he'd stopped her from falling. "I guess it was," she said, smiling.

"I'm Shane." He held out his hand and she slid hers into it.

"I'm—"

"Ban!" A loud voice boomed behind them and they both turned.

Shane released her hand and stood up, a wide grin splitting his face. A shorter man with close-cut blond hair dropped his bag and threw himself at Shane, who grabbed him in a bear hug. He wrapped his legs around Shane's waist and slapped his back with both hands.

"Get off me, you weirdo," Shane said, releasing his friend.

His friend punched him on the shoulder. "You like it weird."

Another man, slightly taller than Shane, joined them. "Way not to make a scene."

He and Shane clasped hands and did the bro-hug, back-slapping thing guys do. "Good to see you, Ban."

"You too, Ghost."

Kinley stared wide-eyed at the trio. Who were these guys? All three were well muscled. The second guy Shane had called Ghost had his hair shaved so short that he might as well have been bald.

"Let's get you guys checked in so we can go," Shane said. He turned and spotted her still sitting in the seats. "Oh. Hey, guys, this is… I didn't actually catch your name."

"Kinley," she said as she stood.

"Kinley," he repeated. "This is Oakley and Ghost." He pointed to each of the men. "Guys, this is Kinley. She's catching a ride with us to Carmelita."

Oakley took her hand in his. "Trust Ban to find the prettiest girl in a place."

She glanced between the three. "I thought his name was Shane."

"It is. We call him Ban because—"

Shane shoved Oakley aside. "That's a story for another time. You two go check in so we can get to the hotel sometime today and not scare our guest within the first fifteen minutes of meeting her."

Ghost grunted and approached the counter and a wide-eyed Francisco.

Oakley leaned around Shane. "I'll tell you the story during the ride," he said in a stage whisper, then dodged Shane's half-hearted swing at him as he joined Ghost at the counter.

"Don't mind them—they're harmless for the most part," Shane said.

"Okay…" What had she gotten herself into? The next couple of hours were definitely going to be interesting.

CHAPTER 2

Shane shoved Oakley out of the way when he tried to climb into the small van behind Kinley. Oakley might be one of his best friends, but he sure as hell wasn't going to horn in on the woman Shane had saved from possible disaster. Twice.

Oakley opened the front passenger door with a low chuckle while Shane climbed into the middle seat. He glanced over his shoulder at Ghost, sitting in the center of the back row with his arms spread out across the back of the seat.

"You good?" he asked.

Ghost gave him a chin tilt, but didn't say anything. Shane smiled, glad to see not much had changed.

The driver got in and turned to face them. "Hola. I'm Jorge. There is water in the cooler here if you get thirsty." He pointed to the small Styrofoam cooler between the driver and passenger seats. "It is one hour and a half to Carmelita. If you need anything on the drive, please let me know." He faced front and started the van, pulling out into the heavy airport traffic.

"Thank you, again, for letting me tag along with you guys," Kinley said next to him. She pulled out her wallet and opened it. "I only have two hundred dollars in cash on me. I can write you a check if it's more than that or I can PayPal you the money."

"It's really no problem. And we're not taking your money," Shane said. "We're headed in that direction anyway."

"Are you sure?"

"Put your wallet away," Oakley said. "Your money's no good with us."

"Thank you." She returned her wallet to her small purse. "What happened to the other guy that was supposed to be with you?"

"What other guy?" Ghost asked from behind them.

"Shane said there was a fourth person who was supposed to be on the trip, but couldn't make it."

"Oh. I lied." He shifted so he partially faced Kinley. "It was pissing me off that he was giving you grief. It wasn't costing him anything to let you ride with us."

"Oh. Well, thank…you. Again." A pretty blush stained the tops of her cheeks.

He grinned. "You're welcome. Again."

She smiled and pulled a notebook and pen out of the small backpack at her feet and flipped to the middle. Taking her cue, he glanced out the window at the passing scenery.

Shane felt Oakley's gaze and looked at him. Oakley made a gesture with his hands like a plane crashing and exploding upon impact. He flipped Oakley the bird.

Sneaking peeks at her during the drive, he noticed the way she pinched her bottom lip between her fingers and furrowed her brow or twirled a lock of hair around her fingers. Occasionally she jotted notes down in the margin of her notebook or flipped back and forth between pages. What was she reading? He tried to read a page out of the corner of his eye, but had a hard time figuring out what the script and block pictures meant.

About an hour into the drive, she stretched her neck side to side, closed her notebook, and returned it to her backpack. "Why…um, what tour are you guys taking?" she asked.

"We're going on a freaking hike," Ghost said.

Shane rolled his eyes. Not this again. Oakley's uneasiness with enclosed spaces had nixed Ghost's caving suggestion and all he'd done since was complain about their "walk in the woods."

"Huh?" Kinley asked.

"What Ghost means to say is that we're taking a nice leisurely stroll to *El Mirador*," Oakley said. "It's more sedate than we're used to, but the whole purpose of the trip is to *relax*." He leaned around his seat to glare at Ghost.

"I'm not sure most people would describe a six-day trek through the Guatemalan jungle as relaxing," Kinley said.

"We aren't most people," Ghost said.

"Who are you then?" Kinley asked.

"We're SEALs," Oakley said.

A pang of regret hit Shane deep in the gut. He heard the pride, and yeah, a little bit of conceit, in Oakley's voice.

"So you're all in the military?"

"They're still active duty," Shane said. "I separated about three years ago and work in private security now."

He hated he had to add "former" in front of SEAL when he told people about himself. His civilian job was great, but it would never compare to being a SEAL.

Kinley shifted in her seat and put her back against the window. "Is that how you all know each other?"

"Yeah." Shane nodded. "We went through BUD/S training together."

"I don't know what that means." Kinley shook her head. "What's buds?"

"Basic Underwater Demolition/SEAL training," Oakley said. "It's where they teach us to be badasses."

Her eyes widened slightly. "Oh."

"What about you, Kinley? Why are you going to Carmelita?" Oakley turned a bit more to face her.

"I'm joining an archaeological dig at a newly discovered Mayan ruin complex."

"You're an archaeologist? That's cool," Shane said.

"Kind of. I'm a crypto archaeologist, not a dig-in-the-dirt kind of archaeologist."

"What's a crypto archaeologist?" Ghost asked.

Shane glanced at him, surprised that he was taking an interest in their conversation.

"I decrypt and translate ancient writing and hieroglyphics," she said.

"So you can read Egyptian hieroglyphics?" Shane asked.

"A little bit, but my specialty is ancient Mesoamerican, specifically Mayan writing."

Smart and beautiful. With her long brown hair pulled into a ponytail, wisps framing her face, Kinley looked like the girl next door. Finding out she specialized in ancient languages was a serious turn-on.

Shane didn't meet too many women outside his work and it was always difficult getting involved with someone from the office. His mind raced forward. How long was she in Guatemala? Where did she live in the U.S.? Would she give him her number?

No doubt, he was getting ahead of himself. She might not even be interested in him. He'd eked out a college degree in kinesiology because he liked to work out and figured it would help him when he joined the military. Book smart, he was not. Unfortunately, he'd always had a thing for smart women.

"Uh. Guys," Oakley said as the van slowed to a stop.

Shane bent and peered through the windshield, feeling, rather than seeing, Ghost do the same behind him.

Four men stood in the middle of the hard-packed dirt road. Three of them held guns and the other held a machete.

"What the hell?" Shane asked.

"*Banditos*," the driver said.

Kinley gaped at the scene in front of her. "What…? How…?" She couldn't form an articulate question, much less ask it. "This is one of the most traversed roads in the country."

The men in the road yelled and gestured.

"They want us to get out of the car," Jorge said, unlatching his seat belt.

Oakley grabbed his arm. "Hang on a sec." He glanced over his shoulder at Shane and Ghost.

Kinley looked at them as panic slid through her veins. Why was he waiting? What other option did they have except get out of the car and do whatever the bandits told them to do?

She caught the look Shane shared with Oakley, followed by his head tilt in her direction. "Let's do what they say."

"You know we can take them," Ghost said.

Shane turned toward the sliding door and looked at Ghost. "Not with civilians in the line of fire." He slid the door open and eased out of the van, holding his hands away from his body.

"Shit. After you," Ghost said.

Kinley spared him a quick glance and then scooted across the bench seat, taking the hand Shane held out to help her from the van. He pulled her behind him and used a hand on her hip to keep her there while he sidestepped away from the vehicle. Ghost languidly unfolded his large frame from the van and ambled over to them as if they'd stopped to enjoy the scenery and not because they were held up at gunpoint.

Oakley joined them as the driver rounded the hood.

"You see what kind of guns they have?" Shane asked in a low voice.

"Yup," Oakley said. "Standard issue M16."

Needing something to do with her hands, Kinley gripped the back of Shane's shirt. What did it matter what kind of guns they had? They were guns. She swallowed hard and tried to control her breathing. It probably wouldn't help their situation if she started hyperventilating. They might be used to having guns pointed at them, but she wasn't. Not exactly the experience she was hoping to have on this trip.

"We doing this?" Ghost asked.

"Let's see what they want first," Shane replied.

What? Doing what? She was so lost.

One of the men gestured with his gun and spoke in Spanish.

"He said to stop talking and move away from the van," Jorge said.

Following the instructions, they moved to the side of the road. Two of the men stayed with them while the other two opened the back of the van and rummaged through the luggage, throwing bags and miscellaneous boxes out of the cargo area.

She leaned her head against Shane's broad back. As long as they didn't take her laptop or notebook, it would be fine. All her work over the last year was in her laptop. She had backups on her cloud drive, but didn't hold out hope that she'd be able to access them while in the jungle, which was why she'd brought it with her. Her notebook had all her notes and research—it was the whole basis to her research. Clothes and shoes and her little bit of makeup were replaceable, but her work was not.

"Kinley," Shane said in a low voice. "When I tell you to run, run for the tree line. Find a place to hide until I find you."

She lifted her head from his back. "What?"

One of the men behind the van shouted something and one of the two in front of their group reached around Shane to grab Kinley.

"Hey!" Shane pushed the guy away. "Run!"

Kinley stumbled back and hit the ground with a low grunt. She crab-walked as she got her feet under her while Shane wrestled with the guy who tried to grab her. Finally finding her footing, she scrambled up and raced for the tree line behind her. A quick glance over her shoulder showed Oakley, Ghost, and Shane fighting with the three men.

The bandit fighting with Oakley hit him with the butt of his rifle, making the blond man stumble back. The bandit looked around, spotted her and ran toward her.

Shit. Kinley pushed through the trees, dodging vines and boulders. About twenty yards in, she stopped and looked around. Shouting came from the direction of the van, but she couldn't tell who was yelling.

Thick vines fell from one of the trees and created a curtain. If she could squeeze in, she might be able to hide.

She parted the vines and turned sideways to step closer to the trunk of the tree. "No snakes, no spiders. No snakes, no spiders," she whispered. There was just enough space for her to crouch on her heels.

A shot rang out. She flinched, squeezed her eyes closed, and tried to sink into a smaller ball. Two more gunshots. Then…silence.

"Please, please, please, please." She didn't know what she was pleading for. For it to be over. For no one to be shot. For Shane, Oakley, Ghost, and Jorge to not be dead.

That last one was selfish, but she didn't want to be left alone with a group of bandits who wanted who knew what. There had only been three shots. Three guys—three shots. What else was she supposed to think?

She listened intently for any indication that someone was coming after her. What would be worse—no one coming after her, or one of the bandits coming after her?

How long should she stay hidden before venturing out to find out what happened? She decided to count to three hundred. Five minutes should be enough time for someone, anyone, to look for her.

At seventy-four seconds a man ran past her hiding spot and stopped to look around in much the same way she had. She peered through the vines and could tell it was one of the bandits. He kept glancing back and forth as if he expected to see or hear her running ahead of him. The space between the vines was enough for her to see out of her hiding spot. If she could see out, could he see in?

What she needed was a weapon. Glancing around, she found a rock slightly larger than her fist. It wouldn't do anything against a gun, but if she could surprise someone and hit them in the head with it, she might stun them enough to continue running.

She looked at the rock in her hand and back at the man. Could she knock him out? She'd never hit someone before. Well, except her brother but she didn't think he counted.

This guy didn't appear to be in any hurry to pick a direction and look for her.

Kinley tightened her grip on the rock and stood slowly. She eased out of the vines, carefully placing her feet down to avoid crunching any leaves or branches. The man turned suddenly and they both froze, surprised. His wide eyes narrowed and he raised the end of his rifle.

"Arrgghh!" Kinley swung her arm wide and smashed the rock against the side of his head.

A dull thunk and the man fell to the ground on his side, facing her. He remained motionless while Kinley stared down at him for several seconds, then looked at the rock in her hand. She dropped it and wiped her hand on her pants.

"Oh my god." Guilt and remorse flashed through her. Had she killed him? No, his chest was rising and falling, so he was alive. A surprising amount of relief swept through her. There was no telling what the man had planned to do to or with her, but she didn't know if she could live with having killed him.

He groaned. Panic flooded her and her arms flapped like a teenager in a horror flick. She kicked out and connected with his crotch. He groaned again, loudly, and curled in on himself.

Okay, not her most graceful moment and she was glad no one

had been around to see her freak-out. She picked up his rifle and looked around. Putting it in her hiding spot might be too obvious and she had no idea how to use it. She grabbed it the barrel and flung it like a throwing axe as hard as she could into the foliage around her. It didn't land far, but she couldn't see it. Hopefully, he wouldn't be able to either.

She glanced around again. Now what?

CHAPTER 3

"Kinley," a low voice called.

More relief, greater than when she realized she hadn't killed a man, rushed through her. "Here! I'm here."

Shane appeared from the right and hurried to her. He looked down at the man on the ground. "You did that?"

"I hit him with a rock and then kicked him in the balls." It sounded absolutely ridiculous. She might as well have said, "I carried a watermelon."

Shane grinned. "Good girl."

Pleasure at what should be ridiculous praise had heat creeping into her cheeks.

"Come on. We need to get back to the van." He took her hand and broke into a jog. "Are you hurt?"

"No. Are you?" They reached the road and the van. The bodies of the other three bandits lay on the ground and blood pooled under at least one of them.

She swallowed hard. "Are they…?"

"No. Only knocked out," he said matter-of-factly.

Was he telling the truth or telling her what he thought she needed to hear?

He wrapped a large hand around her arm and steadied her. "We need to go. The driver's hit."

A little light-headed, she let him lead her to the van. Jorge lay across the seat she had previously occupied. "Is *he*…?"

"No, but we need to get him medical attention quickly. I need you to help Oakley get the bleeding under control."

She blanched and stopped at the door of the van, shaking her head. "I don't know what to do. I barely know basic first aid."

"Oakley will tell you what he needs." He helped her inside and slammed the door closed behind her.

Kneeling in front of the seat, her back to the driver and passenger seats, she stared down at Jorge. There was a lot of blood. The van lurched forward. He groaned and rolled his head.

"Try to get him to stay still," Oakley said from the back row.

She braced one hand against the seat and nodded. "Okay." She could do that. Gently touching his shoulder, she made shushing noises and told him to be still.

Oakley leaned over the seat and ripped open Jorge's shirt, pressing a large wad of cloth over a gash on the side of his abdomen. There was another wound high on the right side of his chest.

"Hold this." Oakley took her hand and placed it over the cloth. "Press hard."

The driver groaned as she applied pressure and she snatched her fingers away.

Oakley grabbed her hands and stacked them on top of each other over the cloth, pressing down. "It's going to hurt him, but we need to stop the bleeding. Press hard." He searched her eyes and nodded, asking if she understood.

Up to that moment he'd been kind of goofy—the kind of guy who didn't take things too seriously. Now he was all business, which only drove home how serious the situation was.

"Okay," she whispered. Trying to remember her high school

biology, she hoped the bullet hadn't hit anything vital. Studying hieroglyphics and dead languages had not prepared her for this.

Grabbing Jorge's pants, Oakley bent the driver's knees so his feet were on the seat and tilted his legs so they rested against the back of the seat.

"This first aid kit sucks," he said. "Did either of you bring your IFAK?"

She glanced over her shoulder at Shane and Ghost, sucking in a breath when she caught a glimpse of the butt of a rifle in the crook of Ghost's arm. They hit a bump and she fell to the side, hitting the arm rest.

"Nope," Shane said from the driver's seat.

"Walk in the woods, remember?" Ghost asked.

Kinley righted herself and reapplied pressure over the wound.

"Right," Oakley muttered, then looked at her. "I don't suppose you have an IFAK?"

She shook her head. "I don't know what that is."

"Individual First Aid Kit. Has all the basics for combat wounds." He looked down at whatever he had on the seat next to him. "All this kit has is Band-Aids and gauze."

"Do the best you can. I think we're ten to fifteen minutes from Carmelita," Shane said. "Hopefully they have at least a clinic and can get him back to Flores quickly."

"Do you have anything plastic?" Oakley asked. "Like a sandwich bag."

"I have the bag my apple was in." What did he need with a sandwich bag?

Oakley put his hands over hers. "Let go."

She pulled her hands from the wound as he took over applying pressure.

"Let me have the bag," he said.

She dug through her pack and pulled out the bag with the core.

"Switch back," he said.

She handed him the bag and watched while he dumped the apple core out. "Lift your hands." He removed the bandages and placed the plastic square over the chest wound, taping the sides down with Band-Aids.

"That will have to do for now." He replaced the bloody bandage. "Keep applying pressure."

"I don't understand how this could happen," Kinley said. "This is one of the most used tourist routes in the country."

"It can happen anywhere," Ghost said. "Desperate people do desperate things."

Maybe, but she still didn't understand what had made them desperate enough to try to hold up a tourist group. The van was clearly marked with the company's logo. She'd heard of tourists being kidnapped for ransom in countries like Colombia and Venezuela, but nothing like that had come up when she'd been researching this trip.

The van slowed almost to a full stop before taking a sharp left and speeding up again. Glancing out the window, she glimpsed wooden fences and corrugated tin roofs bordering the road. The van slowed again as the buildings got closer together.

"There," Ghost said.

Kinley jerked as the van veered to the left and stopped suddenly. Both front doors opened, followed quickly by the side door. Ghost jumped out and rushed into the building they'd parked in front of.

Shane motioned for her to get out and she scrambled out on her hands and knees, moving quickly to the side as he and Oakley lifted the driver out and carried him into the building. She followed and her eyes struggled to adjust to the dim interior of the clapboard building.

A short woman gesticulated and spoke loudly in Spanish while they lay the driver on a bare gurney.

"She says there's no doctor here and we have to…go to Flores," Kinley said. "I think. My Spanish isn't very good."

"He won't make it back to Flores," Shane said.

Ghost and Oakley rummaged through drawers and cabinets. "I've got saline and an IV. And a fourteen gauge," Oakley said.

"Antiseptic," Ghost said. "Nothing stronger than acetaminophen, though."

"Let's get a line started," Oakley said.

"What can I do?" Kinley watched the men work, apparently knowing what to do without discussion, and felt useless. She didn't want to get in the way, but if she could help at all, she wanted to do it.

"Keep pressure on the wound on his side while they work," Shane said. "I need to make a call."

~

Shane stepped outside the building, away from the woman still yelling at them in Spanish, and called the office.

"This is Graham."

"It's Shane." He paced back and forth in front of the door, scanning from one end of the road to the other.

"What do you need?" he asked.

Graham was the reason he'd signed on with Leonidas in the first place and the reason he stayed, even though he was feeling restless.

"I need medevac in Carmelita, Guatemala. An air ambulance would be ideal."

"For you or someone else?" Graham asked.

Shane could hear the keys of a keyboard clicking away while he gave Graham a quick rundown of the attack and driver's injuries.

"Air ambulance is thirty minutes out. Can you stabilize the driver that long?"

Shane inhaled. "We'll do our best."

"Do you think it was random or were you targeted?" he asked.

"I don't think this was about Leonidas." Something was off about the attack, though. They'd focused on Kinley from the beginning. It had all gone to hell when one of the men had tried to grab her. Fear had gripped him as he watched that man chase after her into the jungle, not being able to help her in the moment, hoping she'd be safe until he could get to her. He'd been surprised, and strangely proud, when he learned she'd defended herself.

"All right. Stay alert and let me know if you need anything else."

"Head on a swivel." Shane ended the call and scanned the road again.

It was wide and ran from one end of the town to the other. It might actually be wide enough and long enough to use as a landing strip for small aircraft. Getting back in the van, Shane moved it to the side of the block of buildings. Graham hadn't said whether the air ambulance was fixed-wing or rotary, but he hoped it would land as close to the clinic as possible.

Walking back in the clinic, he found Kinley sitting on a low stool, staring at her hands while Oakley and Ghost fiddled with the IV line.

"Evac is on the way. How is he?"

Kinley looked up. "They stuck a needle in his chest."

Her skin was pale, making the circles under her eyes appear more bluish while her pupils were so wide he could barely see the green of her irises.

Squatting in front of her, he took her hands in his. She had washed them but still had blood around her nails. "It relieves the pressure in the chest cavity created by the bullet wound. You doing okay?"

She shook her head. "I'm not sure. I've never seen that much blood before."

Before he could respond, two men in police uniforms stormed into the small examination room. "Get away from that man."

Shane rose and stepped in front of Kinley, shielding her from the newest threat. Until the men identified themselves, that was exactly how he would treat them. Sparing a glance at Oakley and Ghost, he saw they felt the same even though they had taken a step away from the driver. There wasn't much they could do for him until the ambulance arrived anyway.

"Who are you? Who shot this man?" one of the men asked in heavily accented English.

"My name is Shane Ivers. This man is our tour driver. We were stopped on the road from Flores by four men with guns and he was shot while we were trying to get away."

"You think *banditos* tried to kidnap you?"

Shane pointed toward the end of town. "We were attacked about fifteen minutes from here." He didn't know if the men they injured would still be on the road and it was better not to mention there might be bodies for them to find.

The two men spoke in rapid-fire Spanish, then one of them left. "You will come with me while we check your story," the other said.

"There's an air ambulance on the way to transport the driver to a hospital." Shane glanced at his watch. "It will be here in less than five minutes. I'd like to wait until he's loaded up and on his way."

The officer scoffed. "There is no air ambulance available in this area."

"Maybe not usually, but one is en route," Shane said.

"Fine. Show me your passports while we wait."

Shane glanced at the others who shrugged and shook their heads. "All our identification is in our bags, which are still in the van. It's parked on the side of the building."

The officer widened his stance and crossed his arms over his chest. "Someone will get your bags while you are questioned."

Shane leaned against the wall next to Kinley and matched the officer's pose. No skin off his nose.

A few minutes of tense silence later, they heard the sound of a helicopter approaching. The officer's eyes widened and his arms released slightly. The noise grew louder until gusts of wind blew in the still-open door to the clinic.

The police officer left the clinic and Shane followed. Outside, the civilian equivalent of a military UH-60 helicopter touched down in the middle of the street about fifty yards east of the clinic, its rotors still spinning.

A woman wearing a blue flight suit with a red cross on the breast exited the back of the helicopter and looked around. Shane raised his arms and waved them over his head before jogging to meet her halfway between the helo and the clinic.

"Shane Ivers?" she asked in a loud voice.

"Yes," he said.

"Karen Abbot. Where's the patient?"

He liked that she didn't waste any time on small talk. "This way." He cocked his head in the direction of the clinic.

A man exited the helicopter carrying a collapsible litter and followed them. Stepping inside the clinic, the woman asked, "What's his status?"

Oakley went through the injuries. He'd been shot twice and the chest wound caused a lot of secondary damage.

Karen's companion flipped out the litter and they loaded Jorge onto it, placing the bag of fluids on his chest once he was strapped in.

They followed the medics as far as the door of the clinic and watched while they loaded him. Karen waved before climbing in and slamming the door shut. They all turned their heads and covered their faces with their hands as the helicopter lifted off, its rotors kicking up dust.

"I need a drink," Oakley said.

"You and me both," Ghost said.

CHAPTER 4

"r. Ivers?"

Kinley glanced at the policeman as he approached. Not this again. Raw, gritty tears stung the backs of her eyes—the urge to cry from frustration was strong. Nothing had gone right from the moment she'd set foot in Guatemala. If she didn't want to prove her discovery so badly, she'd walk out of this police station, get in the van, drive herself back to the airport, and catch the next flight back to the U.S.

"I spoke with Mr. Graham from The Leonidas Corporation, as well as the district governor," the officer said.

His tone and demeanor were much more conciliatory than they'd been earlier. Whoever Mr. Graham was, he'd obviously had an effect on the man's attitude.

"We retrieved your bags from the van and have them at the police station," he continued. "We need to record your statements of the incident, but you will be free to go after."

"Of course, Officer...?" Shane held out his hand.

"Pineda." He took Shane's hand. "I apologize for earlier. The nurse is my wife's sister. She said you came in with guns and a man you shot."

"They didn't shoot him!" Kinley's outrage drove her forward a step. "That man would have died if not for them. They very likely saved his life. And mine."

"Of course, Miss… I'm sorry, the man I spoke with did not know who you were," Officer Pineda said.

"Kinley Dunn. I'm with the International Archaeological Foundation."

"Ah, yes," he said. "Many archaeologists pass through Carmelita. I will escort you to the hotel once we are finished."

"We can all find the hotel together." Shane shifted closer to her side.

The muscles in her shoulders relaxed. Shane's no-nonsense statement eased a worry she hadn't even realized she had. Whether it was the way they'd protected her or the intense events of the last couple of hours, the idea of being by herself and not with these virtual strangers was suddenly terrifying.

"Of course. If you will follow me?" Officer Pineda gestured for them to cross the street. Despite his easy tone, she had no doubt it wasn't an invitation they could really refuse.

Forever later, but really in less than thirty minutes, Kinley had both her backpacks and crossbody bag, her passport, laptop, and, most importantly, her notebook. She clutched it to her chest and breathed a sigh of relief.

"Did they break the lock on your diary?"

Kinley opened her eyes and smiled at Oakley as he sat in the hard plastic chair next to hers. "Not quite. All my research is in here."

"Can I?" he asked.

She stared at the simple composition notebook, then held it out to him. "Sure."

He took it gently and opened it, flipping through the pages. He frowned and tilted his head, turning the notebook sideways. "What language is this?"

She glanced at the page he looked at. "Well, the pictures are

Mayan glyphs."

"Okay. What's the rest of it?" He stretched out his arms, then pulled the notebook closer to his face.

Kinley chuckled. "That's my own code."

Oakley closed the cover and returned her notebook. "Do you write all your notes in code?"

"I do." She didn't want to get into the details right then, so returned the notebook to her backpack.

"Who's ready for that drink?" Shane entered the small waiting room, settling his duffel bag on his shoulder, followed by Ghost.

"I need to check in to the hotel and find the Foundation site office. I think it's at the hotel," Kinley said.

"I could do with a shower before we eat," Oakley said.

Shane looked at Ghost. "You?"

He only tilted his head back in a semblance of a nod, which must have been agreement in man-speak.

"All right. Let's check into our rooms and get cleaned up, then food." Shane leaned down and picked up her pack, hefting it over his other shoulder.

"I can... Okay, then." Kinley stared at his back as he walked out of the police station, ignoring her protest that she could carry her own bag.

"Better follow him," Oakley said with a grin.

Kinley sighed and settled her smaller backpack on her shoulder. This was definitely turning into an interesting trip and she hadn't even reached the ruins yet. At least Shane's lean hips and confident swagger gave her something to focus on other than what a catastrophe it was turning into.

∽

"*G*racias." Kinley took the long envelope from the hotel desk clerk. Settling into the worn but clean sofa in the lobby, she tore open the flap and pulled out the single sheet of handwritten note paper.

Kinley, I went to the site a few days early. A car will meet you outside the hotel at 8 a.m. on Friday morning. I'm so excited to share what we've discovered so far! - Christine

Why hadn't she sent the driver to the airport? Or sent her some kind of email or message before she left Carmelita? Kinley had already connected to the hotel's Wi-Fi and checked her email, so Christine should have been able to. Had Christine forgotten when she was supposed to arrive? It wouldn't have taken any longer to send her an email to check in than it had to write her a note.

She slumped back against the couch and pressed her lips together, staring at the paper. Christine had probably forgotten about her. Her nose stung and she twitched it back and forth. It was exhaustion, that was all—not the crushing weight of disappointment. Everything would look better after a good night's sleep.

If Shane and his friends didn't come down soon, she was going to forgo food and settle for sleep, which would be…disappointing. Her stomach flipped at the idea of not seeing Shane again before she left. Of course, she would also miss saying thank you to Oakley and Ghost and saying good-bye properly. Sure, that was all it was.

Not the way Shane had taken care of her all day. Or the way he simply watched her out of the corner of his eye when he didn't think she was paying attention. Or the way he'd been upset when they'd taken her away to be questioned separately at the police station. Or the way he'd carried her bag up to her room and set it inside the door once she'd opened it and made sure she locked the door before he left. Or the way his smile seemed to form in slow motion, reducing her focus to the way his full lips spread into a Cheshire-like grin.

Who really found courteous, chivalrous, sexy men attractive nowadays anyway?

A huge yawn overtook her, causing her jaw to pop. She needed to eat and sleep. Exhaustion was going to win sooner rather than later. According to her phone, it wasn't even six in the evening, which seemed impossible.

"*Centavo* for your thoughts."

"Huh?" She looked up from her phone as Shane sat in the chair to her right. *Wow.* His still-wet hair curled around his ears and his snug T-shirt showed off his muscular arms. Her best friend was always sending her pictures of "arm porn," but Kinley had never understood the appeal until that very moment. Who knew arm hair was such a turn-on?

"Oh. Uh...hey." Giving herself a moment to gather her wits back together, she shoved the letter into her purse. "I was about to give up on you guys and call it a night."

"Sorry about that. I had to make some calls. Jorge made it to the hospital and they got him into surgery. My company will let me know when he's out and how he's doing."

"That's good. Thank you for letting me know." A kernel of shame wormed its way through her. She'd been so distracted by her own problems and thoughts of Shane's arms she hadn't even wondered about Jorge. She was a horrible, horrible person.

"You okay?" he asked. His eyes flitted back and forth as he examined her, tiny lines forming between his eyebrows.

"Yes. Just tired and hungry."

"Well, let's go." He pushed up from his chair and held out his hand, palm up. "Oakley and Ghost can either catch up with us or starve."

Kinley slipped her hand into Shane's. His rough-skinned fingers closed around hers and he exerted the smallest amount of pressure to help her stand as a tingle raced up her forearm.

It felt significant. More than just a helping hand. It was as if they'd struck an unspoken deal, but she wasn't one hundred percent sure what that deal was.

CHAPTER 5

Shane directed Kinley to the small cantina he'd scoped out earlier, sneaking glances out of the corner of his eye while they walked. She looked better than she had earlier but was definitely still pale.

He, Oakley, and Ghost had taken the time to recon the town after dropping Kinley off at her room and making sure she was locked in. After conducting a brief after-action of the assault, they all agreed the attack wasn't random, but didn't know why they'd been targeted. The attackers had been looking for something specific—they just didn't know what. Or who, since they'd tried to grab Kinley after searching their bags.

Inside the restaurant, he led them to a square four-top table in the back of the room. Turning the table so the corner of it faced the wall, he held out a chair for Kinley and took one of the seats facing the front entrance and kitchen. Once Oakley and Ghost joined them, they'd have the entire restaurant covered.

A short, plump woman approached their table.

"*Hola. Agua y menu, por favor,*" Kinley said.

His lips twitched. Her accent really was horrible.

"*No hay menu. Hoy es tamales, pepián de pollo, o hilachas, y arroz,*" the woman said.

He watched Kinley's eyes widen as she tried to follow the woman's rapid-fire Spanish and took pity on her. "She said they don't have a menu. Today's options are tamales, chicken pepián, or a shredded beef dish, and rice."

Her head swung his way. "You speak Spanish?"

Nodding, he watched her emotions play across her face. She should never play poker.

Her rosy lips parted, then pressed together before one corner of her mouth quirked up. "Well, you get to do the translating from this point on."

He appreciated that she didn't throw a fit or get huffy that he'd let her struggle through speaking Spanish. He hadn't done it on purpose—she'd taken the lead whenever anyone had spoken to them earlier and he hadn't seen the need to tell her he spoke it.

"Deal."

"The chicken pepián is a local dish and is supposed to be really good. I'll have that with the rice," she said.

He ordered four servings of the chicken and extra tamales as well as water and beer for everyone. Oakley and Ghost pushed through the low door as the woman returned to the kitchen. They scanned the small restaurant before heading to the table. As soon as they took their seats, the woman returned with drinks.

"I got ahold of the tour company," Shane said, picking up his beer. "The driver was also our tour guide. There are no guides available for the next three days. Our options are to wait or go ourselves."

"I say we go ourselves," Ghost said. "Didn't see the point of a guided tour anyway."

Oakley swallowed his beer with a satisfied sigh. "I wanted a nice, relaxing vacation where I didn't have to think about anything or plan anything."

Ghost cocked a brow. "How's that working out?"

"Fan-freaking-tastic." Oakley raised his bottle and air toasted Ghost before downing half of it.

"Can I ask something?" Kinley rolled her bottle between her fingers.

"Shoot," Shane said.

"How are you guys not freaked out about what happened? I was shaking the whole time I was in the shower."

Damn, he hadn't thought about her going into shock after he left her. "That was your adrenaline crashing. I should have made sure you were okay before leaving you alone."

She shook her head. "I was all right. I didn't expect you to babysit me."

Oakley shifted in his chair and leaned back, affecting a relaxed pose Shane knew was anything but. "That was really nothing."

Shane braced his forearms on the table. "What he means is we've faced more difficult situations."

"How did you know what to do?" she asked.

"Training," Oakley said.

"But you didn't talk about what needed to be done—you just did it."

"Lots and lots of training," Ghost added.

"It was really impressive," she said. "I froze up. I couldn't even remember simple first aid like applying pressure to stop the bleeding."

Shane took one of her hands in his, stopping her from picking at the label on the bottle. When she raised her gaze to his, he said, "It's like any other skill you learn and practice. Take driving. You're probably a much better driver now than you were when you first learned because you practice. Things you used to think about ahead of time, you now do from muscle memory. It's the same idea, just a different skill set."

She nodded at his explanation and he ran his thumb over her

knuckles before letting her hand go. He didn't want to, but it would be awkward to keep holding on. It could have been his imagination, but her fingers tightened ever so slightly before she pulled her hand away.

The woman came from the kitchen holding a heaping plate of tortillas in one hand and a large platter of tamales in the other. They moved glasses and bottles from the middle of the table to make room for the plates. She left and quickly returned with a tray laden with bowls of their food.

"This is a lot of food," Kinley said.

"You think?" Oakley scooped a heaping spoon of rice onto his plate. "I'm already planning on asking for seconds."

Kinley laughed and shook her head. "You can probably have some of mine."

"Oh, we'll eat whatever you don't," Shane said.

"And still ask for more," Ghost said.

They ate quickly with little conversation, everyone concentrating on their plates. Despite asking for more, Oakley and Ghost finished before Kinley was halfway through her food.

Shane shot them a look and tilted his head toward the door.

Oakley spread his arms wide in an exaggerated stretch and yawned. "Oh, man. Would you look at the time. Ghost and I should go and figure out what we're going to do tomorrow. And get some shut-eye. 'Cause…yeah. We're tired."

Kinley looked at the three of them, suspicion pinching her brows and turning the corners of her mouth down. "It's only a little after seven."

"Yeah, but we had a looong day. Delayed flight. Saving the world. Wears a guy out."

Shane shook his head while Ghost chewed on a tortilla and watched Oakley make a fool of himself.

"Well, if you're that tired, don't stay on my account. I can find my own way back to the hotel."

"No, no, no." Oakley stood and scraped his chair back under the table, smacking Shane on the shoulder. "Ban'll keep you company and walk you back. Let's go, Ghost."

Ghost grunted and stood. "Have a good night." He snagged another tortilla and followed Oakley to the door.

Shane signaled for two more beers and relaxed down into his seat, pulling Oakley's empty chair around to rest his arm on the back of it.

"So, Kinley. How are you finding Guatemala?"

She laughed. "It's been way more exciting than I was expecting."

"It hasn't all been bad, has it?"

"No, not all of it."

Deciding not to press any further for the moment, he asked, "Where do you live—when you're not running around Central American jungles?"

"Well, this is a little embarrassing," she said, twirling her bottle. "I've been couch surfing for the past four months or so."

"Why is that embarrassing?"

"Because I'm almost thirty-one years old, have two bachelor's degrees and a master's, and I don't have an apartment or a house or any of the other adult things you're supposed to have by now."

He didn't know if this was something she felt strongly about or if it was something other people felt strongly about and made it known. "Who says you have to be an adult by thirty?"

Her eyes widened. "Everyone!"

"I don't know this everyone, but they sound like real assholes." He held her gaze and drank his beer, challenging her to tell him why she cared about what other people thought.

"No...that's not... You know what I mean."

He leaned forward and rested his elbows on the table. "I don't think having a permanent address is what defines you as an adult. The only reason I have an apartment and am not still living in my kid brother's basement is because he and his wife are expecting and they need the space. Otherwise, I'd still be sleeping on their pull-out."

Kinley rested her chin on her fist. "What do you think defines you as an adult?"

"I don't know. You should probably ask an adult." He winked.

She threw her head back and laughed, exactly as he was hoping. What he hadn't counted on was the way it exposed the long column of her neck and drew attention to the skin of her chest above the V-neck button-down.

"Where do you do all this couch surfing?" he asked.

Her shoulders still shook a little as her laugh died. "Right now, I'm staying with a friend in Raleigh. I'm waiting to hear if I've been accepted to UNC's PhD program."

"We're neighbors." He calculated the drive time. It was four hours to Fort Bragg, so it couldn't be that much more to Raleigh.

"Where do you live?" she asked.

"I'm in Charleston, South Carolina. Mount Pleasant actually, but most people don't know where that is."

"Why do Oakley and Ghost call you Ban?"

He wondered when that was going to come up again. "That's a story for another time when I'm not trying to make a good impression."

She smiled. "Is that what you're trying to do?"

"Yes. Is it working?"

"Maybe a little," she said with a shrug. "Why aren't you married?"

"Who said I'm not?" he asked, teasing.

Her face fell and she leaned back. Immediately, he realized his mistake.

"I'm not." He placed a hand on her forearm. "I'm sorry—I was teasing. I didn't expect you to take me seriously."

"I don't know too many people who would joke about being unfaithful," she said.

"I have a really warped sense of humor, some would even say nihilistic."

She nodded and seemed to accept his answer, even if it was begrudgingly. It felt important that she understood it really was his poor attempt at humor.

"I'm divorced. It was finalized three years ago. Which is when I started sleeping on my brother's couch."

Her eyes filled with concern. "I'm sorry."

"Don't be. It had been over for a while, but it was easier to stay married—especially since I was always deployed. She filed when I had to get out. She liked the prestige of being able to say she was married to a SEAL, but it wasn't about me, it was about my Trident."

She frowned. "Your what?"

"Trident. It's the emblem of the SEALs."

"The eagle thingy?" she asked.

He chuckled. "Yeah. The eagle thingy."

"You said *had* to get out. Did something happen?"

"I blew out my knee. It required complete reconstructive surgery. I recovered enough to stay in the Navy, but not enough to go back to my unit. If I couldn't be a SEAL, I didn't want to be in the Navy."

"I'm sorry." She placed her hand over his this time. "It sounds like you loved it."

He nodded. "I did, but nothing lasts forever. What about you? Why aren't you married?"

She tilted her head. "Who said I'm not?"

Shane smirked, knowing she'd forgiven him for his blunder. "Good one. I'd bet my vintage MG convertible you're not. You don't strike me as the type of woman to linger over the last two tortillas with a guy you just met."

"You're right. I was engaged."

He raised his eyebrows. "Was—but not anymore?"

"No, not anymore. He stole my thesis idea and tried to pass it off as his own."

"Motherfucker!"

Kinley's eyes widened.

"Sorry, but that's a shitty thing to do. Tell me you piled all his shit in the driveway and set it on fire."

"No, but my advisor was on the board and I'd already cleared my topic with her so she knew it wasn't his. They kicked him out of the program."

"Good." He caught the older woman peeking out of the kitchen again. "I think she's waiting for us to leave."

Kinley glanced over her shoulder, then at her watch. "We should go. I need to be in the lobby early tomorrow to meet my ride."

Shane nodded and finished the last of his beer, washing it down with a large gulp of water. The older woman came from the kitchen, a big smile on her face.

"She's very beautiful," she said in Spanish.

"She is."

The woman winked and accepted the bills he handed her. Fanning them out, she tried to give some back.

"No." He pushed her hand back. "Thank you for letting us stay."

Kinley waited for him near the door.

"Can I walk you to your room?"

"Sure." A faint pink stained the top of her cheeks.

Outside, he used a hand on the small of her back to guide her toward the hotel. "How long are you in Guatemala?"

"A few weeks at least." She twisted in his direction while she walked. "It depends on how the excavation goes and how much translation I have to do on-site."

Shane held open the door to the hotel and let her go ahead of him, following her up the stairs to the second floor. "Will you go back to North Carolina after you're finished?"

"Yes, unless I get an offer to participate in another excavation or don't get into the program I applied to. This is me." She stopped in front of a door a few down from his.

"Kinley, can I ask you a question?"

Her pulse throbbed in the small hollow of her throat and, if he had to guess, she held her breath a moment before answering. "Of course."

"May I kiss you?"

Her pupils dilated and the tip of her pink tongue licked her lips. "Yes," she whispered.

He stepped inches closer and eased his hand behind her neck. Bending his head, he pressed his lips to hers. He kept the kiss simple, not trusting himself. If he deepened the kiss, he'd have her pressed against the door with her legs wrapped around his waist in a heartbeat.

Her lips moved under his and he pulled away. Her sigh feathered against his lips, testing his resolve.

"Can I ask you something else?" he asked.

"Yes." Her voice was breathy and a little hoarse.

"Can I have your phone?"

She pulled away and blinked up at him. "Why?"

"So I can give you my number."

"Oh." Her gaze lowered. "Sure." She pulled it from her back pocket and handed it to him.

He programmed his number into her contacts list and sent himself a text before he handed her phone back. "Let me know when you find what you're looking for."

She grinned. "I will. Let me know how you like your hike."

"I will. Good night, Kinley."

"Good night, Shane."

He walked backward down the hall until she unlocked her door and entered the room, closing the door behind her. He fist-bumped the air and strutted the last few feet to the room he shared with Oakley and Ghost.

Pushing open the door, he said, "Guatemala rocks."

Ghost grunted from his twin bed. Oakley looked up from his book, but whatever smartass comment he was going to say was cut off by a sharp scream.

Shane stopped dead. "Kinley."

CHAPTER 6

Kinley pulled her bottom lip between her teeth and smiled, pushing the door closed and throwing the bolt. Meeting a tall, funny, good-looking guy was the last thing she expected from this trip. And that kiss...

Something dark and rough landed on her head and over her face. She flinched and shook her head, trying to dislodge it. A strong band wrapped around her, trapping her arms and squeezing her chest.

Her scream was cut off when something slapped her in the face, hitting her nose and causing tears to well. Her brain finally caught up with her body and she realized someone was attacking her.

"Where is the notebook?" a harsh voice asked.

Even if she wanted to answer, the cloth over her head combined with whatever was pressing against her mouth stifled the air, making it difficult to draw breath. White spots danced in the darkness in front of her.

The attacker picked her up and she kicked out, hoping to strike something or someone, and maybe throw them off-balance.

A huge crash from the front of the room made her attacker

loosen his arms briefly and she twisted her body even more, to no avail. He tightened his hold, but the hood over her head came loose and fell.

Something cold and hard pressed against her chin. A gun. Holy shit. She froze and stared at Shane—the reason for the huge crash judging by the mangled doorjamb behind him.

"Leave or I will shoot her," the man behind her said.

Kinley froze and watched Shane. He appeared remarkably calm.

"Not happening," he said.

A low whistle sounded near her ear and the man behind her screamed, dropping her and the gun. She stumbled a few steps to the side, catching herself on the edge of the bed. In the blink of an eye, Shane wrapped his arms around the man's head and twisted, then dropped the man to the floor.

Kinley could only stare between the body and Shane. Shane and the body.

"Seriously?" He spread his hands wide and glared at Ghost. "You could have hit her."

Ghost grabbed the handle of the knife and pulled it from her attacker's shoulder, wiping it on the man's shirt. "Not likely."

"You killed him," she said.

"Yeah," Shane said.

"He's dead."

"It was you or him, honey," Oakley said from the doorway. "We need to go."

Shane grabbed her upper arm and pulled her toward the door.

"Wait!" She reached between the mattress and the box spring and pulled out the travel sleeve which held her laptop and notebook, then grabbed her pack from the chair next to the bed.

Shane took her pack and shuffled her down the hall to their room. Oakley closed and locked the door, pushing a chair under the handle as an extra precaution.

"Shouldn't we call the police?" Kinley asked.

"Not this time," Ghost said.

"There's no such thing as coincidence," Oakley said.

"Agreed." Shane shoved clothes into his brown duffel.

Kinley's gaze jumped from one man to the other, trying to keep up. "What's not a coincidence?"

"The carjacking. This attack. They're looking for something," Shane said.

"The question is, what do they want?" Ghost asked.

Blood pulsed through her body and her ears felt like they were stuffed with cotton. She looked down at the case cradled against her chest and worked her jaw side to side.

"This." She unzipped the case and pulled out her notebook. "They're looking for my notebook."

"Why?" Oakley asked.

Kinley took a deep breath. "I'm not a hundred percent sure, but I think it's because I deciphered the Lago Azul text."

Two...three seconds of still silence. "You say that like it's important," Ghost said.

"The Lago Azul texts predate current deciphered Mayan texts by two to three hundred years," she said. "They've never been deciphered until now."

"Okay," Shane said. "I can see why that would be a big deal, but why would someone try to steal it?"

"Because within the text is what people believe are directions to a fabled Mayan city—the same city I'm supposed to go to tomorrow."

"Why would someone try to steal a book with a map for a city they'd already found?" Ghost asked.

Kinley sat on the edge of one of the beds and rubbed her forehead, trying to ease the pressure building behind her eyes. "There's a myth about a powerful Mayan ruler named Aapo who poisoned and killed all his people and then buried himself with his earthly riches so he could take them to the afterlife with him. The myth says the burial chamber is at the very center of the great pyramid of this city and the key to opening the burial chamber is contained in the Lago Azul text."

"Which you deciphered," Shane said.

She pressed her lips together and nodded.

"How many earthly riches?" Ghost asked.

"All of them," Kinley said. "Basically the Mayan version of Croesus."

Oakley leaned over to Shane and stage-whispered, "Who's Croesus?"

Shane shrugged.

Kinley couldn't stop the small smile. "Think El Dorado, but ten times bigger."

Oakley and Shane nodded and looked suitably impressed. The illusion was ruined when Oakley leaned over again and whispered, "How big was El Dorado?"

Shane pushed him away. "How many people know you broke the code?"

"My mentor, and she shared the sample I sent with all the team leads because some of them didn't think I'd really done it," Kinley said.

"How many people is that?" he asked.

"Five or six. More if they passed the information on to their assistants or other people in their departments."

"So, anyone who knows you broke the code could be behind this," Ghost said.

Her shoulders sagged. "Yeah."

Betrayal and dejection warred for top spot on her emotional ladder. Was this because someone was greedy and wanted all the glory for themselves or because she, a basic nobody, had translated texts that preeminent Mayan experts in the world had been unable to translate?

"Do you think the story about the rich Mayan guy is true?" Oakley asked.

Kinley shrugged. "The myth of El Dorado lasted centuries and no one ever found it. It's probably the same with this one."

Shane looked at the window then strode over to it. The other two men joined him and they gathered around, peering through the curtains.

"What is it?" Kinley asked.

"Three large black SUVs," Shane said.

"Those are nice cars," Ghost added.

Oakley nodded. "Too nice for a little town like Carmelita."

She joined them and peeked around the edge of the curtain. A woman got out of the back of the middle SUV.

Kinley gasped. "That's Christine."

"Who?" Shane asked.

"Christine Banks—my mentor. She was supposed to pick me up at the airport this morning but never answered any of my calls." Had it really only been this morning? It seemed like days ago that she tripped over Shane's bag. "She left me a note at the hotel telling me a car would pick me up tomorrow morning."

A tall, well-dressed man exited the vehicle behind her and took her elbow. He gestured and shouted directions at the other men exiting the vehicles.

"That man was at the airport," Kinley said.

"Are you sure?" Shane asked.

"Yes. He sat next to me after I called one of the other professors. He said he overheard my conversation and offered to bring me to Carmelita."

Christine pulled away from the man and he grabbed her arm again, pushing her against the car and wrapping his hand around her throat.

"She doesn't look like she's all that happy to be here," Oakley said.

Kinley's brows furrowed. "No, she doesn't."

"We need to get out of this hotel," Ghost said.

Shane couldn't agree more. He was only just starting to form a picture of what they were up against, but priority one was to get Kinley away from it.

"Grab your gear," he said.

"What about...?" Kinley pointed out the window.

Shane glanced out again in time to see one of the police officers from earlier in the day jog over to the man who'd grabbed Kinley's friend.

"I'm not exactly sure what's going on, but I do know it's never a good idea to turn yourself over to the bad guys." He slung his duffel over his shoulder. "Especially when the local cops are involved."

"Roof access is to the right at the end of the hall," Ghost said.

"I've got point," Oakley said.

"Go," Ghost said. "I've got your six."

Shane grabbed Kinley's hand in his and glanced out the door to the left in the direction of Kinley's room, then followed Oakley to the right. The door to the stairwell was cracked and he eased it open, glancing up the stairs in case Oakley had run into any issues. A low whistle indicated the all clear and he led Kinley up the concrete steps to the roof.

Very few lights illuminated the street below them, making it difficult to find Oakley in the dark. Shane finally spotted him crouched close to the low wall at the side of the building.

"All the buildings are roughly the same height with only a foot or two gap between them," he said. "If we travel across a few, it should get us far enough away from the tangos before we hit the ground."

"We're going to jump across the buildings?" Kinley asked.

Shane could see the whites of her eyes in the dim light. "Hey. It'll be okay. I've got you. We all do. We'll get you across. Trust us."

She hesitated, but nodded and whispered, "Okay."

He shifted his duffel bag around to his chest so the strap crossed his back. "Give me your backpack."

She slid it off her shoulders and he loosened the straps before slinging it over his back. "That'll make it easier."

"We good?" Ghost asked.

Kinley nodded, much more confident than the first time.

"We're good," Shane said.

He was able to straddle the space between most of the buildings and help Kinley step from one low wall to the next. Only twice did they need to find something to span the gap to walk across. The second time, Oakley backtracked to get the wide plank of wood they'd used the first time.

Kinley crossed without complaint or balking, even when the plank had shifted under her weight. He wanted to give her an *attagirl*, but his boss would probably fire him if she ever got wind of it, so he simply smiled his encouragement.

They'd crossed seven buildings before they reached the cross street and had to descend to the ground. They hunkered between the last two buildings on the street.

"Now what?" Oakley asked.

"We should go back to Flores," Kinley said. "I'll contact the Foundation and let them know what's going on."

Shane exchanged a look with Oakley and Ghost. She wasn't certain about the idea. "I hear a *but*," he said.

She remained silent, chewing on the edge of her thumb, and glanced toward the street.

"Do you want us to talk you into that plan or out of it?" Oakley asked.

"If we do that, I'll probably be taken off the excavation. I'll have to turn my notes over to someone else." She paused and chewed on her nail again. "Dr. Banks could be in serious trouble. The sensible thing to do is alert the authorities."

Oakley huffed out a laugh. "No one ever accused any of us of being sensible."

Shane didn't think she was leaning toward going to Flores and contacting the authorities, but if he told her it was the right thing to do, she'd do it.

Maybe it was wishful thinking. Maybe he was jonesing for his old life so bad, he was looking for a chance to do something "operational." Maybe it was selfish, but he wanted Kinley to choose option B. "If you want to find out if the burial chamber is real, we'll help you do it."

"I want to find out if it's real," Kinley whispered.

"I'd rather go treasure hunting than follow a fucking hiking trail," Ghost added.

Option B it was. A sliver of remorse wormed through his conscience. Her eyes shone with so much excitement and trust, he almost took his offer back. Almost.

"Let's go find your dead guy's treasure."

CHAPTER 7

"Did you take the granola bar out of my bag?" Oakley asked.

"No," Ghost said around a mouthful of food.

"You dick. That was my last one," Oakley threw an empty water bottle at his. "I'm starving."

"So was I," Ghost said.

"Then you should have packed your own food!"

"I did. I ate it."

"Asshole."

Leaning against the metal wall of the small storage shed they'd found on the outskirts of town, Kinley watched the two men fight. Was this what it was like to have brothers? She had two sisters and they had been in some knock-down, hair-pulling, screaming fests when they were growing up. She always told them their parents should have traded them for boys. She should probably call and apologize when she got the chance.

Shane sat down on the floor next to her. "Can you tell us some more about this lost city?"

"Yeah. Of course." She turned to face him more fully. *Don't get distracted by his mouth, Kin.* She rubbed the sleepy grit from her eyes. "The ruins were found using LIDAR. It's a method of surveying that uses pulsed laser light to illuminate an area and then the reflected pulse is measured with a sensor. It's kind of like how sound waves—"

Ghost waved his hands and formed a T. "I know you're in sharing knowledge mode, but it will probably save you some time to tell you we know what LIDAR is."

Heat suffused her neck and cheeks and she glanced down at her hands. "Right…sorry."

"Ignore him," Shane said. "He's an ass on the best of days, but doubly so when he's hangry. How about if you explain like we understand everything and we'll ask questions if we need to?"

She smiled, still flustered after Ghost's interruption, but continued. "Sure. Imagery showed that the Mayan civilization was much more extensive than previously thought. The site that was discovered may even be a separate civilization that predates the Mayans by almost five hundred years. It changes everything archaeologists thought they knew."

"What about that Blue Lake text you figured out?" Oakley asked.

"The Lago Azul text." She pulled out her notebook and pulled out the copies of the text. "Here, look. The inscriptions are different from classical Mayan inscriptions. Some of the glyphs had been translated, but not most of them, so it was hard to put into any kind of context. One of the deciphered glyphs is the symbol for sun, since it's very similar to the classic Mayan glyph for sun. A lot of scholars believed the text is part of a ritual worship of the sun god—kind of like a prayer. But I think what most scholars have translated as 'sun' actually means 'enlightenment.' See these two little additions on the side of the glyph? I think they work similar to diacritics in the Arabic alphabet where it changes the sound of the consonant, only in this case it changes the meaning of the word."

"Why is that important?" Oakley asked.

Kinley shook her head and shrugged as a yawn stretched her jaw wide. "Sorry. I don't know. I don't have enough expert knowledge about Mayan culture to say whether it's important or not. That's one of the reasons I was so excited to be working on this excavation with Dr. Ford—she's one of the foremost experts on Mayan culture and history."

"Do you have any maps of the area?" Ghost asked.

She dug into her bag, feeling for the large plastic file folder, and pulled it out. Releasing the elastic holding it closed, she pulled out the colorful LIDAR images of the area and handed them to Shane.

He glanced through them, then passed them to Ghost. "You don't have any topographical maps?"

"No. I figured the team would have maps, so I didn't bother with any. The only reason I have these is because there's something about the layout of the city that's teasing at the corner of my mind and I can't figure it out."

Shane's phone buzzed. "Ivers…yeah, got it."

He disconnected the short call. "We need to get some wheels. We have a rendezvous in six hours. They're going to have gear and maps for us. And food."

"Huh. Maybe the private sector isn't such a bad gig," Ghost said.

"Let me know when you're ready to punch. In the meantime, there's also a ride for you two to Belize."

Oakley sat up straight. "Do what?"

"You're still active duty. The last thing you guys need is to go traipsing through the jungle, getting hurt."

"First of all," Oakley said, "I don't traipse—whatever the hell that is."

"Second—you do know what we do for a living, right?" Ghost asked.

"Yeah. Which is why you don't need to get injured, killed, or worse—court-martialed—if shit goes south."

Kinley had to wonder about guys who considered getting court-martialed worse than dying. She watched the silent exchange between Ghost and Oakley.

"Fine," Ghost said. "But if I'm hanging out in Belize to finish my leave, you better tell your guy to make reservations at a beachside resort."

"You sure this is the place?"

Shane didn't fault Ghost for asking. "This is where the coordinates are."

The small village was more like a group of huts than anything else, although in the early morning light he might have described it as picturesque. Pulling the beat-up car off the road, he stared at the small building through the rearview mirror.

"Are we here?" Kinley asked from the back. She'd passed out almost as soon as they'd loaded up in the car.

"Looks like it," Oakley said.

"Take your bags," Shane said. No sense in coming back for them if this was the place and better to have them than have to leave them if it wasn't.

They approached the house slowly, taking note of the surroundings and keeping Kinley between them. Two wire-haired dogs slept under a rough-hewn bench by the door. Shane knocked softly on the wooden door and it swung open, revealing a dimly lit interior. Stepping over the threshold, he scanned the sparsely furnished open room. A table and three chairs stood against one wall, with a cold firepit to the left, and a door leading to another room on the right.

"This better not be the resort," Oakley said.

"It's not," a woman said.

Shane pushed Kinley behind him and faced the threat. It took a second to register the woman stepping out of the doorway to the other room wasn't a threat, at least not to him. Maybe. It was always kind of hard to tell and depended on her mood at the moment.

"Jesus, Paige. Give a guy a heart attack, why don't you? What are you doing here?"

She leaned against the door frame, crossing her arms. "I was the closest."

"I didn't know we had a job down here," he said.

"We didn't." Her voice was the audible definition of disgruntled. "I was on vacation."

"Anywhere good?" Ghost asked.

"Turks and Caicos."

"Nice," Ghost said. "We should go there."

"You're already booked at an all-inclusive in Belize. I'll be dropping you off at the Guatemala City airport on my way back to my vacation." She straightened from the doorway and looked at Shane. "We need to talk."

He ran his hand down Kinley's arm. "I'll be right back."

Following Paige into the room, which had a small platform bed and not much else, he closed the door behind him. "What's up?"

She raised one perfectly arched eyebrow and crossed her arms. "What are you doing, Shane?"

He really didn't like this side of Paige. She gave a stare down worse than anyone he'd ever met. Even his mom when he'd gotten caught trying to sneak out of the house in high school to go meet up with Kiki White.

"What? I'm helping Kinley."

"And when did you meet Kinley?"

"Yesterday."

"So we're expending funds and favors because you want to impress a girl?"

"It's not like that, Paige." It wasn't. It was more than wanting to impress Kinley or even find that temple she talked about.

"Then explain what it's like. Because I was enjoying myself on the beach and now I'm being eaten alive by mosquitos." She slapped at her arm to emphasize her point.

Running his hands through his curls that no amount of gel or product could tame, he summarized the events of the last day.

"Why can't we turn this over to the authorities?" Paige asked.

"Kinley's afraid if we turn this over to the authorities or go to the foundation she's working for, she'll get taken off the team."

Paige stared at him, assessing him, fucking reading him in that uncanny way of hers.

"I need this, Paige. For the first time since I blew out my knee, I feel like I have a purpose. I know this isn't a mission, but this whole situation is… I can't explain it." Not in a way that would make sense to anyone else, at least. He felt…alive. Like he could breathe deep.

She sighed. "Do you need a team with you? I agree it's not a good idea for your buddies to be here—there are too many things that can go wrong. It's a slow week at home, which is why *I* was on vacation, so I can have a couple guys here in a day or two."

All the expected tension left his body, even with her dig at being pulled away from her trip, and he relaxed his shoulders. His biggest fear was that Leonidas wouldn't provide support. He could manage on his own, but it would be harder.

"I've got it covered for now."

Paige lifted her chin a fraction in agreement. "I'm going to stage Devon, Harrison, and Jordan in Flores. They'll attract less attention in a bigger city. I've also got Angie digging into any back chatter she can find so we can have some kind of idea of what group or groups we're dealing with. I'm telling you now, if I think this is too much for you to handle on your own, I'm sending the team in."

She opened the door and left the small room. That had gone better than he expected. He thought she'd drag them all back to the airport and tell them they were idiots. The fact that she already had Leonidas's cybertech specialist looking into it meant she'd never intended on pulling him off this mission…case…adventure. It didn't matter what he called it. Right now, it was his purpose.

He followed Paige out of the room and found Oakley, Ghost, and Kinley gathered around the small table while Paige hefted a large pack onto it.

"You have a GPS and satellite phone as well as sleeping bags and camping gear," she said.

"And rations." Oakley held up an MRE.

"We are definitely going to the resort," Ghost said.

Paige held up a large square of paper. "There are also maps of the area."

He took a map and unfolded it, spreading it out on the table. Kinley already had the LIDAR images out and laid them over it.

"The images aren't the greatest since I got them from the internet, but this should be the temple," Kinley said, pointing at a bright square.

"I'll send the coordinates to the team so they know where you're headed." Paige pulled out her phone and tapped on it with her thumbs. "You're safe in the house and village, but don't linger for more than a day or two."

"We'll set out at first light," Shane said.

"All right. There's a four-wheel-drive parked behind the house. Keys are in the center console. We'll take the vehicle you acquired earlier and leave it somewhere along the way," Paige said. "Be careful, Shane. Call the team *before* you need them ASAP."

His lips quirked up. "Thanks, Paige."

"Don't thank me—I was going to leave your ass here. The only reason I came is Graham agreed to cover the cost of my resort." She waved over her shoulder.

Shane grinned after her. She was so full of it. She wouldn't leave anyone out to hang. Give them shit for an eternity, sure, but she'd be the first one into the fray if one of the team needed it.

Ghost and Oakley stopped in front of him.

"Kind of feel like the job is only half done," Ghost said.

Shane clasped his hand and pulled him into a one-armed hug, slapping him on the shoulder while Ghost did the same. "There's always another job."

"Yeah. Next time let's go right to the all-inclusive."

He left and Shane and Oakley hugged it out.

"Lot of effort to get the girl," Oakley said. "Hope you're worth it." He winked and followed Ghost and Paige, pulling the door to the house firmly shut behind him.

CHAPTER 8

Kinley watched as Shane tore the top off the smoking bag and pulled the dark brown pouch out of it, setting the still smoking bag off to the side. Smoking—not steaming. The chemical pouch in the bottom of the bag produced a toxic smoke, but apparently it was perfectly fine to heat their "meals ready to eat" with.

"You're sure these are okay to eat?" she asked.

"Oh yeah. These are downright gourmet compared to what we used to have." He used a knife to cut the side off the pouch he held. "The trick is to cut along the length instead of ripping across the top. That way you don't have to shove your hand into the pouch to get to the bottom of it."

"This is my first MRE," she said.

"What do you normally eat when you're on digs?"

Heat crept up her neck and she lowered her gaze. "This is my first real trip to the field."

"Really?"

Kinley nodded. "I've been on training trips, but they were to established sites—Egypt and Pompeii. My concentration has always been glyph translation, not the actual digging part.

Honestly, the only reason I was invited on this trip is because I translated the Lago Azul text."

She took the pouch and spoon he held out to her and poked at the food before taking a small bite of what she assumed was meat. Not bad. Saltier than she liked her food, but it wasn't horrible even if it was unevenly heated through.

"Stir it around a bit," Shane said, opening the other pouch.

She moved the food back and forth and took another bite. That was better. At least the cold spots and hot spots were mixed together.

Shane passed her a water bottle and held his up. "Here's to your first real dig."

"Thanks." She tapped her bottle against his then guzzled half before she realized it. The food was really salty.

"What do you think?" he asked.

She shrugged. "It's not bad."

He grinned at her. "You can be honest."

"Well, I wouldn't eat it every day." Poking at her food, she peeked at him through her lashes. "Can I ask you something?"

"Sure."

She rested her arms on the edge of the table. "Why are you helping me? You barely know me, but you called your company and they're expending all these resources to help me find a treasure that probably doesn't even exist. Why?"

Shane flipped the spoon over in his mouth and slowly pulled it out. He probably wasn't purposely trying to distract her from her question, but watching the plastic slide between his lips made her breath catch and her nipples pucker behind the thin shield of her bra.

"That's a multipart answer," he said.

"What?" She blinked.

"Why we're helping you." The twinkle in his eye told her he'd caught her ogling his mouth.

She cleared her throat and sipped her water. "Right. So why?"

"I've traveled all over the world. Every time I visit some historical landmark, I wonder what it must be like to be the person who discovered it. To be the first person to see something that hasn't been seen for hundreds or thousands of years."

Her inner nerd sighed with happiness. That was about the most perfect response, but it didn't answer her question. "I understand that, but why are you helping *me*?"

He leaned forward and stared directly into her eyes. "I don't like people being taken advantage of, or attacked, or cheated out of something. You deserve the credit for this find."

The intensity in his hazel, gold-flecked eyes was too much and she had to look away. "If we find it."

Shane leaned back and scooped food out of his pouch. "When we find it. Besides, I *really* don't like being shot at."

Kinley huffed out a laugh. "Thank you. For the ride, for saving me—both times—for doing all this. I won't ever be able to repay you or Oakley or Ghost or Paige for everything you've done. I don't know what would have happened if I hadn't fallen on you."

Maybe even falling for him. Wouldn't that be monumentally stupid?

"I think you would have figured it out," he said.

"Do you do this a lot?" she asked

"Camp out with beautiful women?" He grinned. "No. You're much better looking than my normal travel companions."

She smiled, despite the blush she felt on her cheeks. "No. This kind of…mission, I guess."

He shrugged. "Sometimes. Not as much as I did when I was active duty. Now I mostly do personal security. Leonidas will sometimes get a subcontract with the military, but we haven't had any since I started working for them."

"You mentioned Leonidas before—what is that?"

"The Leonidas Corporation. It's the company I work for. Paige is one of the owners. She's the Chief Operations Officer. She and my other boss, Graham, run the company."

"Do you like it?" she asked. "I don't know too many companies that would go to all this trouble for someone, especially a complete stranger."

"TLC is the closest I've come to feeling like part of a team since I got out." He put his spoon in the empty food pouch and stuck it in the trash. "It's more than just a business for Graham and Paige. They built the company from the ground up, hand selected everyone that works there. We all have some kind of connection to one another."

Shane stopped and blinked, frowned a little. He looked like someone who'd just realized something that had been staring him in the face.

Kinley slid her hand over the top of his. "It sounds like a really great place to work."

He nodded. "It is. And you're right. None of the other companies I worked for before Leonidas would have been down with this. They sure as hell wouldn't have supported it."

"Well, I for one am glad you're working for them and not one of those other companies," she said.

"Me too."

Her gaze dropped to his mouth again, his firm lips tipped up at the corners giving him a boyish, devil-may-care charm. He turned his hand over so her palm rested against his and his thumb rubbed back and forth across her wrist. The moment stretched on, each of them silently waiting for the other to…what? Make a move? Break the spell they seemed to be under?

Kinley had a feeling she was too far out of her depth with a man like Shane Ivers. His easygoing, surfer-next-door look hid an intensity she'd never experienced. He was completely still except for his thumb, brushing gently across the sensitive skin of her wrist. But she knew it was a façade. If she gave any indication that she was willing or uneasy, he'd react in a heartbeat. The problem was, she didn't know if she wanted him to let her go so she could swim to shore, or pull her under and devour her.

Her own indecision decided for her and he eased his hand out from under hers. "There's a small bathroom off the bedroom. You should grab a shower and get some sleep. It's going to be a long day tomorrow."

"Right. Of course." She pushed away from the table and gathered up the trash from their dinner.

Shane took it from her. "Don't worry about this, I've got it."

"No. I helped make the mess, I should help clean it up." She wanted to hide her embarrassment without making it look like she was trying to escape to the bathroom.

"It's not a lot," he said.

He was right. He had most of the trash in a small bag before she finished her argument. "Okay. I just need my—" She stepped left and forward as he stepped to the right and their bodies knocked into each other.

Kinley didn't know who moved first. All she knew was his back under her hands was as wide and hard as it looked and his hands grasping the back of her head were strong and demanding. And his lips… Dear god, his lips were lush and firm and warm against hers. His tongue brushed the seam of her mouth and she opened under him, tangling her tongue with his.

Waves of desire coursed through her body. She'd never been so affected by a kiss. She wanted more. Like an alcoholic teased with a sip of whiskey, she wanted the whole damn bottle. She ran her hands down his back and found the edge of his shirt, sliding her hands back up the hot expanse of skin. He groaned and she flexed the tips of her fingers into his back.

His hands traced either side of her spine until they reached her hips and he pulled her even closer, nestling his erection against her stomach.

Emboldened, her hands skimmed down his back to his firm ass and squeezed.

His fingers dug into the flesh on her sides and he groaned. "We should stop," he said, breaking the kiss and resting his forehead against hers.

Straining her eyes to look up at him, she found his closed. His chest heaved against hers and his rough breath feathered her lips.

"I don't want to." She tried to press her lips against his, but he stopped her by gently holding her head.

"This is just a reaction to everything that's happened. It's normal to want to reaffirm life when you've been in danger." He still didn't open his eyes, so it wasn't clear if he was talking to her or himself.

"Is that what you and Ghost and Oakley would do after a mission? Reaffirm your lives?"

That got his eyes open. "What? No."

"I'm not judging." She shrugged. "I understand how it could happen, especially with people you trust with your life. What's more trusting than an intimate moment?"

His eyes jumped back and forth as he searched her gaze. "You're giving me shit, aren't you?"

Kinley cracked a smile. "Yes, I'm giving you shit. If you think you're reacting this way because your life was in danger, okay. But I still don't want to stop."

Shane grinned and then his face returned to serious. "If you change your mind, just tell me and I'll back off."

"I'm not going to change my mind." She ran her hands up his stomach and chest, letting her fingers map the ridges and dips. "You saved my life. You're going on this search with me..."

He dropped his hands from her waist and stepped back. "You don't have to trade sex as a thank you."

"That's not... You didn't let me finish. I'm attracted to you. Physically. If I wasn't, I wouldn't be doing this. That you did those things—that you're doing those things—makes you as attractive on the inside as you are on the outside."

Licking his lips, he closed the distance between them. "So you think I'm hot?"

Kinley shook her head and smirked. Of course that's what he would take from her little speech. "Yeah. You're hot."

He cupped her jaw between his hands again. "As long as you're not doing this for the wrong reasons."

"Is there ever a wrong reason to have sex with a hot guy?" she asked.

"I don't know. I've never had sex with a hot guy."

Kinley laughed and stood on her toes to kiss him. She'd never tried to kiss someone while he or she was smiling. It felt almost more intimate than a regular kiss.

"Bedroom?" he asked.

"Bedroom."

Shane walked backward, pulling her across the small room to the even smaller bedroom. Clothes and shoes flew everywhere while he kissed each area of exposed skin. Kinley cursed the practical sports bra she'd put on because it meant Shane had to lift his head from her chest while she pulled it over her head.

He cupped her breasts before she was even clear of it. As soon as she wrapped her arms around his head, he sucked a tight nipple into his mouth. Her clit pulsed as her core clenched, seeking relief.

"Your tits are gorgeous," he said, moving from one to the other.

Kinley bit her lower lip between her teeth. Her nipples were so sensitive, driving her arousal even higher. "Bed," she said.

"Hang on." Shane lapped at her breasts one more time before he returned to the other room.

Dropping her panties to the ground, Kinley pulled back the blanket and thin sheet from the bed. Lying in the center of it, she massaged her breasts roughly, the way she liked, while her legs moved restlessly on the mattress.

"Fuck me, that's hot."

Kinley cracked open her eyes and found Shane standing next to the bed, holding a strip of condoms in one hand and his erection in the other. His hand stroked up and down his length. He wasn't overly long, but he was thick. She licked her lips and rose to kneel in front of him. Bending at the waist, she pushed his hand aside and sucked him into her mouth, using her tongue to trace the underside of his cock. Relaxing her throat, she could almost take all of him without triggering her gag reflex.

Shane palmed the back of her head, but made no effort to pump into her mouth, letting her do all the work. She appreciated his restraint. She liked giving head—liked the power it gave her—but having a guy who understood the subtleties of letting a woman work her magic was even better.

"Fuck, Kin, that feels good." His words came out as a sigh. "Too good. I don't want to blow my load in your mouth the first time. I want to feel your sweet pussy squeezing me tight when I come."

Hell, with an invitation like that, who was she to say no? Swirling her tongue around the underside of his head before releasing him, she picked up the strip he'd dropped on the bed and tore off a square.

Shane took it from her and opened it, rolling the thin circle down his length.

"No." He stopped her from lying on the bed. "I want to play with your tits while you ride me."

He laid down and settled her on top of him. Kinley wasn't shy by any means but being on full display brought out every single one of her insecurities. The roundness of her stomach gave evidence to her love of chocolate. The outside of her hips had stretch marks from a sudden growth spurt when she was fourteen that no amount of cocoa butter or aloe could ever erase.

"Fuck, you're gorgeous." Shane's fingers dug into the globes of her ass, sliding her back and forth over the length of his cock resting against his abdomen. His gaze traveling down her body felt like a physical caress. Edging his hand around her hip, he rubbed the pad of his thumb through her folds and around her clit.

Just like that, she was firing on all cylinders again. Rising up on her knees, she grasped his erection and positioned herself over it. With a gasp at the first intrusion, she released her weight letting the burn and stretch determine her speed. Fully seated she paused, letting her head fall back and bracing her hands on his thighs.

He'd bottomed out and her whole lower body clenched around him.

Shane grunted as if in pain.

She raised her head. "Are you okay?"

"No." He bent his knees behind her and braced his feet, pushing her back to lean against his legs. "You feel so goddamn good all I want to do is drive up into you until I come so hard, I go blind."

"Okay," she said. "But without the going blind part."

He smirked up at her. "I'm not making any promises. Ride me, Kinley."

She swiveled her hips, rising and lowering. The burn had disappeared, replaced by the torturous push and pull of his cock. True to his word, he cupped her breasts, squeezing and releasing in time to her movements.

"So beautiful," he whispered.

Her orgasm built quickly. Every time she dropped down and circled her hips, his cock head hit the front wall of her channel and her clit rubbed against his pubic bone. When he pinched her nipples between his thumb and finger, there was no stopping the spasms of release.

"Ah!" She sank into him and rubbed back and forth, bracing her hands on his shoulders while she tried to keep the waves of pleasure going.

He shifted under her and grabbed her hips in a punishing grip, raising and lowering her while he thrust up to meet her each time she came down. Then he flipped her onto her back and wrapped her legs around his waist.

"Hold on." He crushed his mouth to hers while he drove into her.

She curled one hand around his shoulders and the other into

the soft curls at the back of his head. A second orgasm took her by surprise and she threw her head back.

Shane dropped his head into the curve of her neck and thrust hard, staying there as his body shuddered.

It was several minutes before their breathing returned to any semblance of normal. Kinley still had her arms and legs wrapped around Shane while he peppered her neck and shoulder with soft kisses. She didn't want to let him go.

"Are you blind?" she asked.

His body shook with laughter, shaking her and the bed along with it. He lifted his head and brushed a strand of hair away from her face. "No, but I did see stars." He kissed her on the lips and pushed up, going into the small bathroom and closing the door.

Kinley stared up at the underside of the thatch roof. Yeah…so did she.

CHAPTER 9

Shane tugged on the vines and branches, doing his best to cover the Jeep at the end of the so-called road they'd managed to follow that far. "It's probably three full days on foot from here to the edge of the ruins."

"Yeah."

He glanced sharply at Kinley, concerned by her distracted tone. They'd set out before the sun had risen over the horizon and hadn't said much to each other. Definitely nothing about what happened last night. He shouldn't have let it go so far, but when her lips had touched his, all rational thought about doing the right thing had flown out of his head. His big head, because the little head had taken over all conscious thought after that.

Thankfully she appeared engrossed in the maps and imagery spread out on her pack, turning them one way and then the other, glancing occasionally at her notebook in her other hand.

"What's wrong?" he asked.

"I don't know." She turned the map ninety degrees and cocked her head in the other direction. "There's something…" She shook her head. "I'm missing something, I just don't know what it is."

He squatted next to her and picked up a sheaf of papers. A

photograph of Mayan hieroglyphs carved into stone was on top. Each page underneath appeared to be different sections of the same carving until he reached the last page, which showed the whole stone.

Shane picked up the LIDAR imagery and compared it to the picture of the carvings. "Huh. They're the same."

"What?" Kinley asked.

"The ruins and this carving are laid out in the same pattern." He held the pages side-by-side. "See?"

"Oh my god." She dropped her notebook. "Oh my god!" Taking both of the pages, she plopped down on her ass and crossed her legs. "How did I not see that before?"

"Too close to it," he said. "Sometimes you need to back away or get a fresh pair of eyes on it."

She looked at him with a huge smile, her eyes bright and happy. He might actually give up his car if it meant seeing that look again. Kinley dropped the pages and lunged at him, taking him down with her exuberance.

Clasping the sides of his head, she pressed her mouth to his. She probably only meant it to be a quick thank you kiss, but as soon as he felt her lips, Shane got carried away again.

His arms wrapped around her waist and back and he plunged his tongue into her mouth. A moment's hesitation, then she groaned while circling her tongue around his. Shane's hand slid down her ass, his fingers dipping between her cheeks.

Her legs fell to the sides of his hips and she rocked against him. Only the loud growl of a howler monkey brought him back to reality.

"Fuck." He let his arms flop away and dropped his head into the dirt.

Her head pressed against his breastbone. "I didn't mean for that to happen," she said.

"I know. It was my fault—I got carried away." He stared up at the thick canopy. The only thing that would make this moment worse was if that monkey shit on his face.

She pushed off him, back to her seated position. "I didn't exactly protest or tell you the middle of the jungle floor wasn't the place for a quickie."

Shane heaved up and smirked. "Probably didn't think trouser snake was something you had to look out for, huh?"

Kinley blinked at him and rolled her eyes, but he saw her fighting a smile.

"All right, show me what got you so hot and bothered," he said.

"Right." She pulled the sides of her ponytail. "You're right—the Lago Azul text and the city are laid out in the exact same pattern. Which might be one of the reasons so many scholars had a hard time deciphering the text since it couldn't be read in the normal way." She tilted her head side to side. "But that also means my translation is likely incorrect."

"Why do you say that?" he asked.

"Well, I based my translation on the accepted method of reading classic Mayan text, making allowances for it not being in the standard columns, but if the layout of the text matches the layout of the city, I probably missed something."

"Like what?"

"Like…I don't know. Take this symbol for instance. This part of the symbol means sun." She circled the lower right corner of the square glyph with her finger. "This is what I was talking about before. With these two symbols added to it, I think it changes the meaning to enlightenment not sun, but it could really just mean sun."

Shane pulled his knees up and rested his arms on them, clasping his hands together. He had no idea what she was talking about and yet he was fascinated—and not just with watching her lips move.

"Okay. Why is that important?"

Kinley shrugged her shoulders. "I don't know. It probably isn't.

It's probably another calendar foretelling the apocalypse." She lifted her head. "We should go back. This was silly. I have no idea what I'm doing or what I'm talking about."

He hated seeing the doubt in her eyes. She tried to hide it, but he saw the shimmer of tears as well. Taking her hand in his, he threaded his fingers through hers. "If that's what you want to do, that's what we'll do. It's still early—we can make it back to Flores before dinner."

She gave him a small smile and looked back at her notebook. A small furrow appeared between her brows while her gaze darted between the imagery and the picture of the text. She looked up at the sky, then back down at the map. Slipping her hand from his, she pointed to her left.

"East, right?"

"Yes," he said.

"So that's north." She absentmindedly pointed in that direction, then turned the maps so they aligned with the cardinal directions, mumbling to herself. Her head snapped up and she stared at Shane with excitement back in her eyes.

He smiled. "Figure it out?"

"I don't know. I figured something out."

"Yeah? Want to share?" He scooted closer to look at the maps.

"Okay, bear with me—I'm still working it out in my head."

"Will do."

"The Mayans built their pyramids in much the same way the Egyptians did—almost perfectly aligned with the sun or some other celestial marker. At Chichen Itza, the temple is aligned so perfectly that during the equinoxes it looks like a serpent is slithering down the steps of the temple."

"Okay, I'm with you so far."

"If you look at the position of the temple on the map, it matches up with this symbol on the text which I'm pretty sure means life. Which makes sense because the temple was the center of Mayan culture and their day-to-day life. The sun or enlightenment symbol on the text matches up with this building right here." She tapped the spot on the imagery.

She looked at him expectantly, but he wasn't connecting the dots. "You lost me. Why is that significant?"

"What if the burial chamber isn't in the pyramid? What if it's here?" She shook her head, grinning. "I still think the text describes the path to enlightenment, but I think it's an *actual* path instead of an esoteric way to enlightenment. Why else would they draw the text in the same pattern as the city? And if it's an actual path it would lead to the source of enlightenment. Right?"

"It makes sense to me. Does that mean you still want to follow this path?"

Kinley nodded. "Yeah, I do."

"All right. Let's go."

Shane plotted the coordinates of the location in the city Kinley was so excited about and sent them, along with their current position, to the team on standby in Flores to keep them informed of their progress. He'd send them an update when they stopped for the night.

If they could maintain a decent pace throughout the day, they might be able to make it before nightfall the day after tomorrow. If he was alone, he could probably make it there by sundown tomorrow, but he needed to set his pace based on Kinley's capabilities.

Checking one more time to make sure the Jeep wasn't too visible and that everything was packed up, he looped the compass over his head, programmed the coordinates into the GPS, and hung that around his neck as well.

After finding their heading, he looked at Kinley. "Let's go."

It took him a bit to get back into the rhythm of land navigation, but once he found his groove, he set a steady pace using a machete to clear a path for Kinley to follow.

"Why do you use the compass if you have the GPS?" Kinley asked.

Dropping the compass to his chest, he folded the map and stuck it in the cargo pocket of his pants. "Habit and a precaution. If we lose satellite coverage because the canopy becomes too thick, I don't want to waste a lot of time orienting our position."

He sipped water from his hydro pack, then held the hose out to Kinley. "Drink."

His dick stood up like it had been called to attention when she wrapped her lips around the valve and sucked on it. Yeah…it was going to be an uncomfortable hike.

They set off again, Shane in the lead hacking a path through the jungle while Kinley followed. Every time he glanced back to check on her, she was only a few steps behind watching her feet or him, in which case she'd give him a happy smile.

God, he missed this. Not the sweltering, wet heat of the jungle, but setting an objective and finding the way there through the unknown. His mind and body were in tune and focused in a way they hadn't been in longer than he could remember. Ever since he'd blown out his knee, it was as if he'd been looking at life through a fogged-up lens—the center was in focus, but the edges were hazy. Now it was like looking at everything in high-definition Technicolor.

About two hours into their hike, Kinley had slowed down, increasing the distance between them. They entered a small clearing—he could have stretched his arms out and almost touched the trees on either side—and Shane decided it was as good a place as any to rest and refuel.

Using the machete, he made sure the ground was clear. "Set your pack down and sit on it."

Wet tendrils of hair stuck to her temples.

"Let me see your back," he said after she'd dropped her pack to the ground.

She turned around, revealing the back of her soaked shirt.

"Sit." He dropped his own pack and rummaged in the front

pocket, pulling out an electrolyte packet. Filling it with water, he swirled it around and passed it to Kinley. "Drink this."

She took a gulp then scrunched up her face and stuck her tongue out. "That's disgusting. What is it?"

Shane laughed. They were gross. "It's a sports drink on steroids. You're losing a lot of water and you need to replenish your electrolytes so you don't get dehydrated. Do you need to pee?"

She shook her head.

"That's not a good thing. I want you to take a large sip of water every ten minutes while we're walking."

She nodded and choked down the rest of the electrolyte mix. "How far have we gone?"

"A little more than four miles, give or take."

"That's it? It feels like it should be more than that."

Smiling, he said. "We're doing about fourteen hundred meters every twenty minutes."

"What is that in miles?"

He did the math in his head. "Eight-tenths of a mile, I think. We do all our pace count in meters since it's easier to calculate than miles." He pulled out a packet of crackers and cheese, passing them to Kinley. "Next best thing to gourmet."

She took the food from him. "Huh. I need to go to the gym more."

"I've been setting a pretty fast pace. I can slow down if you need me to."

She shook her head. "I'm okay."

"We have a few more hours before we'll camp for the night. We'll rest again in an hour or so, but if you need to stop before then, let me know."

"Okay." She ate the cracker and looked around their little rest stop.

"What?" he asked.

"I have to go now and I'm not looking forward to squatting in the jungle."

"Oh. Hang on." He unzipped several pockets before he found the item he was looking for. "Here."

Kinley took the thin cardboard triangle. "Thanks. What's it for?"

"It's a funnel." At her blank stare, he said, "So you can pee standing up."

Her eyebrows raised and she pressed on the sides of the cardboard, opening up the funnel. "Why do you have them?"

"Paige included them in all our go bags so she doesn't have to try to squat with all her gear on. I've only ever had to do it a few times, but it's not fun." He paused, realizing he was talking about taking a shit with the girl he liked. "They're biodegradable, so you can leave it when you're done."

"Cool."

They each went to different sides of the clearing, Kinley walking a few extra steps into the brush to relieve herself. With the possible exception of his mother and sister when he was little, he could honestly say he'd never peed around a woman before—not even his ex. They'd always done their private business in private. He didn't feel any discomfort or embarrassment or need to hide the fact that he was human and had bodily functions like every other person on earth. It was weird at the same time it was comfortable.

They set off again, Shane keeping the same pace as before. When he offered to take another break, Kinley waved him off and told him she'd rather get as far as they could that day, although she did accept another electrolyte packet with a grimace as well as a granola bar.

As the light faded, Shane kept an eye out for a suitable spot to make camp. Finding a spot slightly larger than the one where they'd taken their break, he cleared the area of branches and underbrush as best he could for the tent.

"It's going to be tight." He stepped on the anchor with his heel to drive it into the ground. "We can't leave anything outside the tent."

"Why?" Kinley asked.

"Snakes. Spiders. Wayward monkeys."

She stared at him with wide eyes and a horrified look. He didn't know which of the three creeped her out the most. For him it was spiders. Not exactly an arachnophobe, but there were only so many camel spider encounters one person could have before developing a healthy desire to avoid them.

"It'll be fine," he said. He unrolled the sleeping pads and sleeping bags and positioned their packs in the corner of the small tent.

Backing out of the opening, he told her, "It's MREs again tonight."

"Okay." Kinley sounded like she was fading fast.

"Why don't you wait inside while I get everything ready?"

She nodded and crawled into the tent.

"Soup's on," he said about ten minutes later. He peeked into the opening of the tent when he didn't get a response from Kinley. She lay on her side with her head propped in one hand, but her eyes were closed.

Shane shook her foot. "Kinley."

Her head fell off her hand and she jerked up. "Huh?"

"Eat something before you go to sleep."

"'Kay."

He passed her one of the entrées and watched as she half-heartedly ate, barely able to keep her eyes open. She passed on anything else and lay back down in the tent, asleep in seconds.

Shane smiled and untied her hiking boots, pulling them off and setting them on her pack. He cleaned up the remnants of the MREs and shoved it all into the pocket of the pack he'd designated for their trash.

Zipping up the tent behind him, he stripped down to his

boxers and lay facing Kinley. She'd kept up with him like a champ, even though she'd been dragging at the end.

He moved a piece of hair away from her face. Her eyes fluttered and she sighed in her sleep. What the hell was he doing in the middle of the jungle helping a beautiful woman find a lost city? His gut told him he was exactly where he was supposed to be. He'd been lost before, wandering aimlessly without a purpose. Today it felt like he'd found his way and it had nothing to do with the city at the end of the compass.

But everything to do with the woman right in front of him.

CHAPTER 10

Kinley woke with a numb shoulder, something heavy draped over her, and a stick poking her in the back. All reasons camping had never been her thing. Opening her eyes, she confronted the tan fabric of the tent mere inches from her nose. The stick pulsed against her back.

Not a stick—a trouser snake.

She smiled sleepily and nestled her ass against the warm, hard body behind her. She'd always been comfortable asking for what she wanted in bed, which had been one of the many problems with her ex. He thought she should just lie there and be grateful for what he was giving her instead of critiquing his technique. Not that he had any.

Shane on the other hand—he had technique to spare.

A low rumble vibrated against the back of her neck and his hips pressed into her ass. The arm over her waist lifted and he unbuttoned her pants, which she'd fallen asleep in, and dove into her waistband.

She moaned low as he cupped her and pressed from the front and back, one of his fingers rubbing small circles through her underwear.

"How far do you want to go, Kin?" he asked against her neck.

"Far," she said. "So, so far."

"Take these off." He pushed against the front of her pants with his arm, then pulled it out of her pants.

Wiggling her hips, she shoved them and her underwear down to her thighs as she felt him sit up behind her. Kinley rolled to her back and pulled her pants off inside out as Shane grabbed a condom from his pack.

"Back on your side," he said, lying down again.

He slid an arm under her neck and shoved his hand into her sports bra, cupping one breast.

Kinley gasped and turned her head, seeking his mouth. His tongue mated with hers as he ran a hand over her hip and thigh while he slid his cock between her slick folds.

"Shane," she gasped.

He lifted her leg over his and entered her from behind.

"Oh god." She reached blindly for a leg or hip—something to hold onto.

"You're so beautiful. Hot and wet. I can feel you all around me, squeezing me."

His words were punctuated by his strong, leisurely strokes and it was driving her insane.

"It's all I can do not to flip you over and drive into you, but I want it to last. I want it to drive you crazy until you blow all around me." He spoke against her neck, licking, sucking, and nipping between words.

"Stop talking," she said.

"Does it make you hot?" He sucked on the tender lobe of her ear, and shivers of pleasure raced down her skin.

"Yes. If you want it to last, you need to be quiet."

"So you can concentrate on feeling me slide in and out of your tight, hot pussy? So fucking good. I can feel you pulling at me like you don't want to let me go." He flicked her clit and that was it.

"Oh. Fuck! Shane!" Her orgasm powered through her and she

bore down while he pumped into her hard until he buried himself balls deep and scraped his teeth along the column of her neck.

The slight sting sent a smaller orgasm crashing through her, chasing the tail end of the first one.

Kinley's breathing eventually returned to normal while Shane brushed his lips over the spot he'd bitten. She couldn't have stopped the satisfied smile if her life depended on it. What a way to wake up.

Her stomach rumbled. "I'm hungry," she said.

He laughed and squeezed her hip as he slipped from her, leaving an emptiness behind. Then he leaned up on an elbow and tilted her face to him. "Let's get cleaned up and I'll see what I can do.

~

Kinley pushed the vine away from her face and sipped from the valve of her water bladder. Her goal for the day was to avoid drinking that gross, super sweet, fake lemonade crap Shane kept shoving at her. He'd forced one on her before they set out and that was more than enough for the day as far as she was concerned.

Sweat crept down the small of her back. Her hiking pack helped absorb most of it, but there was nothing to stop the steady trickle into the crack of her ass. The pack was too bulky for her to reach the small of her back to rub the spot and keep it from dripping down.

As enjoyable as their activities were that morning, she was starting to regret it. Cleaning up with baby wipes hadn't been exactly refreshing and now, with all the sweat, she could smell herself. This wasn't what she'd envisioned when she'd pictured herself marching through the jungle to be one of the first people in thousands of years to set foot in an ancient Mayan city. The only thing keeping her from turning around and calling it quits was her determination to prove she'd done what everyone said she couldn't have.

The view of Shane's butt ahead of her didn't hurt either.

Her stomach grumbled even though it had only been a couple of hours since they'd eaten breakfast. She'd devoured the MRE Shane had handed her including the crackers and peanut butter that could be used as mortar if they had to build a hut.

"You good back there?" he asked.

"I'm here." He looked like he was barely breaking a sweat as he swung the machete in front of him to clear the path for them. "Do you have any granola bars handy?"

He stopped and turned. "Hungry?"

"Yes, which is weird for me since I don't usually eat more than a couple of times a day."

"You also don't expend this much energy in a day either. Your body's telling you it needs fuel." He swung his pack around and pulled a snack bar from one of the pockets. It was the equivalent of Mary Poppins's carpet bag for backpackers. "Here. This one has more calories—it's still a few hours until lunch."

Shane's head tilted back and Kinley followed his gaze, but only saw the jungle canopy. "What is it?"

"Shhh. Listen."

All she heard were the trees swaying in the light breeze that didn't reach them on the ground, the insects, the birds, and the occasional monkey calling out. Nothing that hadn't been making noise two minutes ago.

She cocked her head, straining to hear anything else. Then the whir of rotor blades reached her.

"What is it?" she whispered. Silly question—he couldn't see any more than she could.

He didn't make her feel stupid for asking, though. "Don't know. The Leonidas team is still in Flores—I checked in with them this morning." He looked back at her. "Whoever it is, they're headed the same direction we are."

The bite of food in her mouth turned to thick paste and she drank water to help swallow it. The picture of Christine being shoved against the car flashed through her mind.

She'd been so selfish, so caught up in the adventure and idea of finding the answer to the riddle, she'd forgotten about the danger they might be facing.

Shane tilted her head up with a finger under her chin. "Hey. Don't do that. It could be a coincidence. There are a lot of places that helicopter could be going."

Kinley swallowed hard. "What if I'm making the wrong decision? What if by not going to the authorities, I've put Christine in even more danger?"

He pulled her into a hug, his arms around her shoulders. She wrapped her arms low around his hips and rested her head on his chest. Why didn't he smell like he'd been trudging through the jungle for hours after having hot monkey sex?

"Paige has a team back in Charleston looking into it and tracking down the information we were able to give them. They'll find answers faster than the local authorities will. That being said, we can turn back anytime you want to."

"Am I completely deluded to think we can do this?"

"No, you're not," he said.

"What are we even going to do if we find anything?"

"Well, I don't know what the proper procedures are, but we take pictures and send them back to Leonidas. Our IT person is scary smart and she'll be able to figure out who should get them."

She nodded her head. That made sense. Or maybe it was complete bullshit, but she wanted to be convinced.

"Can I ask you something?" Shane asked.

Her stomach flipped for reasons that had nothing to do with her worries. "Of course."

"What do you want to get out of this?"

Did he mean the two of them or finding the ruins? "What do you mean by this?"

"Finding this temple or whatever it is."

Ah, so not them this. She hid her disappointment by turning her face further into his chest. "People don't take me seriously. They take one look at me and assume I couldn't possibly know what I'm talking about. How could I? I'm too pretty to be smart." She couldn't hide the bitterness in her voice.

"Has someone actually said that to you?"

"That or some version of it. Christine sent out an email to the team letting them know I'd translated the Lago Azul. One of the PhDs responded that there was no way *I* could have deciphered it because I didn't have the education or experience. He didn't realize I was in the cc line."

"That guy's a dick."

She huffed out a small laugh. "Yeah. Which is why I want to prove him wrong. My translations are going to be important—I just want the chance to prove it."

Shane didn't respond for several moments. Had she shared too much? Did he think she was too ambitious and out of her league?

"Here's what we're going to do," he said. "We're going to get to that temple or house or whatever it is and you're going to translate the hell out of it and then we'll find that PhDick and you can shove it in his face."

Kinley laughed and pulled away. "I like that plan."

"But." His face grew serious. "If I think the threat is too high, we're going back to the village and I'm calling the team in to get us. Okay?"

"Okay." Her pride wasn't worth her life.

"You ready to go again?"

Hitching on the straps of her pack, she shifted its weight higher on her hips. "Let's do it."

CHAPTER 11

They repeated the same routine as the day before, stopping for lunch for about forty-five minutes before setting out again. Shane stopped more frequently to look at the map and check the compass but she didn't know if he really needed to or if it was a ruse to give her a chance to catch her breath. She really needed to consider going to the gym more often when she got home.

Late in the afternoon, Shane stopped and looked around while he consulted the map.

"What is it?" she asked. Based on their spot last night, there didn't appear to be enough room to set up camp where they were.

"Do you hear that?" he asked.

Kinley cocked her head. "Is it another helicopter?"

"No. It sounds like water. There's nothing on the map, but it's not like the jungle has been fully explored." He shoved the map back in his pocket. "Come on, I think it's this way."

Water might mean a bath. Even rinsing off would be heaven.

They broke through the trees at the rocky edge of a wide river. A few feet up hill and up river, a ledge of rocks created a four-foot-high water fall in the otherwise calm water.

"It doesn't look too deep," Shane said. "We should be able to cross with no issues."

Kinley looked up at the darkening sky. "Should we wait until morning when there's more light?"

He shook his head. "I'd rather be able to dry our clothes and boots tonight than hike in wet socks and boots tomorrow. Trench foot and blisters are no joke."

That made sense.

She followed him downstream until he found a spot for them to cross. Kinley picked her way across the hip-deep river, thankful for the moving water. Still water meant leeches. Leeches meant gross.

They walked back upstream to a small dirt-packed area close to the bank.

"This area is probably under water during the rainy season, but it's a good place to set up camp for the night," Shane said.

Putting up the tent was sweat inducing work and Kinley stared longingly at the river, the setting sun glinting off the water in the spots not shaded by jungle.

"What is it?" he asked.

"I'm contemplating taking a bath."

"Go for it," he said.

She didn't have any eco-friendly soap or shampoo, but what the hell. Even just rinsing off would be heavenly. She pulled off her hiking boots without unlacing them, shucked her T-shirt, wet socks and shorts, then walked into the water while Shane laughed behind her.

She did not care and sank down to her chin with a sigh. It was heavenly. The water was cool and swirled around her limbs, carrying away the damp stickiness that had been an almost constant companion for the last few days.

On the bank, Shane gathered her discarded clothes and placed them in the tent before he stripped and walked into the water.

She bit her lip at the sight of him striding toward her naked, a half erection jutting out from between his legs. He stopped in front of her. The water only reached his upper thighs. His cock twitched as if seeking attention.

"You forgot to take this off." He ran a finger under her bra strap.

"Skinny dipping felt indecent," she said thickly. In the cool water, her nipples puckered almost painfully.

"Hmm. Tilt your head back and get your head wet." His voice was low and rough.

She was soaking wet and it had nothing to do with the river. Holding his gaze, she dipped her head back and pulled the elastic from her ponytail. Then she lifted her head and slicked water away from her eyes.

Shane threaded his fingers through her hair at the base of her neck and massaged her scalp.

Her eyes slid shut and she groaned as his strong fingers rubbed her head. Moving her hands through the water, she found his warm, firm thighs, and opened her eyes. His hard cock was right in front of her.

He stared down at her with heavy eyelids. "How does it feel now?"

"Absolutely obscene." She flicked the tip of his erection with her tongue, then slowly slid her mouth over the bulbous head.

His fingers clenched her hair, pulling almost painfully. Unable to move her head, she slid her hands up the back of his thighs to his ass and pulled him forward, forcing him deeper into her mouth.

"Fuck." He unclenched his fingers, which gave her room to move.

Maintaining eye contact, she gripped the base and slowly withdrew. He kneaded her scalp again and she matched her motion to his, sliding up and down his shaft in time to his fingers rubbing back and forth.

Desire suffused her body. It was the hottest moment of her life.

"Damn it. I'm gonna come fast. If you don't want it in your mouth, tell me."

A sense of power flowed through her, heightening her own hunger. She was on her knees in the middle of the river, but she held all the control. She slid her mouth down as far as she could, almost to the base, and sucked as she pulled up to the head.

She wanted him at her mercy. She wanted to take him to the brink and force him over the edge.

"Son of a motherfucker." He pushed his hips forward and tilted his head, closing his eyes. "You like my cock in your mouth, don't you. You like having me at your mercy."

Kinley picked up her pace, hollowing her cheeks as she slid up. The water felt electrified, sparking over her skin and sending a craving shooting through her body.

His ass cheek clenched under her other hand and his fingers gripped tight in her hair. He shuddered and groaned, head falling back as warm come filled her mouth. She swallowed and pumped with her hand and mouth, urging him on.

His fingers relaxed and went back to rubbing small circles on her scalp. She lapped at his softening erection, then kissed her way up his happy trail to his belly button.

He grasped her under her arms. "Up."

She stood and barely had her feet under her before he grabbed her ass and picked her up.

"Give me your mouth."

Kinley grabbed the back of his head and did as he demanded. She wrapped her legs around his waist as he turned in the water and waded back to shore.

In front of the tent, he broke their kiss. "I'm glad I gave you lots of time to rest today."

"Why's that?" she asked breathlessly.

"Because I'm going to wear you the fuck out."

God, she hoped so.

Kinley shoved her dry but stiff clothes into her backpack. She would never take a washing machine for granted again. She'd assumed the dig site camp would have some sort of laundry tent, even if it meant hand washing her clothes, and had packed accordingly. Her only choices that morning had been the somewhat clean and stiff undergarments from the day prior, or smelly, ripe underwear from the day before that that. Somewhat stiff and clean it had been.

"Kinley!" Shane rushed through the edge of the jungle. "Come here. You need to see this."

"What is it?"

He grabbed her hand and pulled her up. "You'll see."

She followed him into the tree line several feet from their camp to a large stone structure.

"Oh my god." She stared reverently for several moments before walking around it. Standing about eight feet high, it was a pillar carved on all four sides. Although weathered and worn, the structure was mostly intact even with small plants sprouting from some crevices.

"It's beautiful."

"Can you read it?"

She walked around it again, paying closer attention to the carvings. "The glyphs look similar to the carvings from the Lago Azul text, not contemporary Mayan carvings. It may be connected to the lost city. I need to take pictures. Shit."

She patted her empty pockets. "My phone and camera are in my bag."

"I'll grab our stuff. You can get pictures and then we'll set off from here."

Kinley walked around the structure and brushed dirt and moss from the glyph carvings. She traced the carvings. It was here, right in front of her. It was only a small sampling of glyphs, but it felt like she'd discovered a whole world.

As soon as Shane returned, she dug her camera out of her bag and walked around the pillar documenting it in full and zooming in on portions she found particularly interesting.

She finally lowered her camera. "Can you mark this location?"

"Already done," he said.

She beamed at him and impulsively snapped a picture of him.

Late in the afternoon, Shane stopped in another small clearing and looked around. "We'll camp here tonight."

"Isn't it kind of early?" Kinley asked.

"Yes, but we're about a quarter mile from the edge of the ruins and I'd rather get there at full light than as it's getting dark."

In only a couple of days they'd established a routine to set up camp. Shane set up the tent while Kinley cleared a spot for a fire and gathered firewood. She stood on the edge of their little clearing, watching Shane drive the tent peg into the ground with the heel of his boot.

He glanced over his shoulder and caught her watching. "What's that look for?"

She dropped the pile of sticks next to the spot for the fire. "I was just thinking that this felt really comfortable. Familiar. Like we've been doing this longer than two days."

"Huh." He looked up vacantly for a moment, then joined her. "It has only been a few days. You're right—it feels much longer than that."

"Is that weird?" She chewed at her lip. She was feeling a lot. For him. For their adventure. Was it the close proximity driving her emotions or Shane?

He rested his hands on her hips. "Sometimes you meet people you click with immediately. It's like you've known them your whole life. It was like that with Ghost and Oakley. More than a hundred guys start training and only about twenty percent make it through. I think a lot of the reason we all made it through was the fact that we clicked from day one."

He pressed a quick kiss to her lips. "So no, I don't think it's weird. We click."

A slow smile spread across her face. *We click.* It wasn't a declaration of love, but after that explanation, it felt more meaningful. Hell, a declaration of love or that they were meant to be would have freaked her out. But saying they clicked, like he'd clicked with his two friends, that felt real.

While Shane prepped their MREs, she flipped through the pictures of the structure he'd found that morning.

"Figure it out yet?" he asked.

"I think so, but it doesn't make sense," she said.

"Why?"

"Well…I think it's a stelae, but those were traditionally built in the cities. There was no evidence of a settlement though." She cocked her head. "Unless the settlement is gone and that's all that's left but…that doesn't make sense either."

He held out a pouch of food. She set her camera next to her and took the food then grabbed a spoon from the packet.

"What's a stelae?"

"It's kind of like a monument to a ruler. It was used to document important events during that ruler's life. Like a stone biography."

"Could it have been put up as a marker for something?" he asked.

She thought about it while chewing on a meatball. "Maybe. Some archeologists believe they were also used as altars. One of the carvings is reminiscent of carvings depicting Ixazalvoh."

"Who's that? A ruler?"

"The divine mother, goddess of water, life, and weaving."

He chewed thoughtfully. "It was close to that river. Could it have been an altar to her?"

"It's possible." She poked at her noodles and sighed. "I wish I could talk to Dr. Banks about this. She'd probably know exactly what it was."

"Hey." He ran a hand over the back of her head. "You have the pictures. You'll see her soon and you'll have so much to share with her."

She smiled and leaned closer, giving him a soft kiss. "Thank you."

"You're welcome," he said softly.

Several hours later, Kinley was wide awake in the dim light cast by the glow stick Shane had snapped earlier. Her mind wouldn't shut off, even though her body was exhausted. She kept picturing the stelae, then visualizing the layout of the city based on the LIDAR imagery and trying to picture where they would enter. Realistically, she knew the jungle would have overtaken the ruins decades ago, but still she envisioned reaching the ruins as they would have been thousands of years ago when they were still in use.

Shane pulled her back against his front, but she stopped his hand from traveling to the juncture of her thighs.

His head lifted from behind her. "You okay?"

She glanced over her shoulder at him. "Will you get angry if I say no?"

"Angry?"

She could hear the confusion in his voice. "Not angry...upset."

He pushed up onto his elbow and turned her onto her back. "Kinley, I'm not going to be anything other than horny and disappointed if you don't want to have sex."

"It's not that I don't want to, I do. It's just…"

"Just?"

She took a deep breath. "I felt funky all day and I know I stink and need a real shower. With soap and not just water." Heat gathered on her cheeks as she remembered how unbath-like her time in the river had been.

A wide, teasing grin spread across his face. "So you're saying you have a serious case of swamp ass?"

"Of what?"

"Swamp ass. When it's hot and your ass is sweaty and kind of ferments in your drawers."

"Eww. That's disgusting and entirely too accurate."

Shane chuckled as he lay back down and pulled her close to his side. "It's worse when it's a barracks full of guys."

Kinley wrinkled her nose. She didn't even want to imagine.

"Try to get some sleep," he said. "Plenty of time tomorrow to worry about tomorrow."

CHAPTER 12

Shane eased his arm from under Kinley's head. She snuffled a little but didn't wake up. Not that he expected her to—she was exhausted.

He shoved his feet into his boots and laced them tight. Grabbing the GPS and night vision goggles that had been an unexpected surprise, he eased out of the tent and crouched outside after zipping it closed to make sure Kinley stayed asleep.

Adjusting the head strap for the NVGs, he switched on the power and infrared illuminator. The jungle lit up like the Las Vegas strip. Maybe not quite as bright, but he could see as well as he could during the day. He quietly moved away from the tent.

Twenty minutes later, a bright spot appeared ahead of him and he slowed his pace, taking care where he set his feet. The jungle would probably cover any inadvertent sounds he made, but it was better to be careful.

A few meters closer to the light, he hit a break in the jungle and crouched down, taking in the scene before him. Someone had cleared a large swath and set up camp. Four large tents circled a fire and he could see at least two people walking around.

Through the jungle overgrowth, Shane could make out the

silhouette of a large pyramid rising above the camp. He pictured Kinley's excitement and regretted not sharing the initial moment with her, but he needed to know what they were walking into before he led her there.

The structure Kinley wanted to explore was on the far side of the pyramid, away from the camp. They could circle around and approach from the north without being seen. He had no way of knowing whether the people in the camp were friendlies, so it was best to avoid them.

∽

Shane stood on the edge of the deep ravine with his hands on his hips, cursing to himself. Damn it. They were going to have to backtrack and edge around the campsite in order to access the far side of the pyramid.

"It's not that big of a deal," Kinley said. "What's a few more hours of walking?"

He gave her a tight smile. He hadn't told her about finding the camp so she didn't know that it was a little bit of a big deal.

They walked another fifteen minutes before he paused to take another bearing to get them around the pyramid.

"Oh my god," she whispered.

"What?" He looked up in time to see her pushing through a fall of vines. Shit, they'd gotten closer to the pyramid than he'd thought. "Kinley, stop."

"Look! It's right here!" She glanced back at him just as a shot rang out, echoing through the jungle.

Kinley let out a short scream. Grabbing the back of her shirt, Shane yanked her to the ground, praying they didn't land on a fer-de-lance. He'd rather be shot than be bitten by a viper.

"Stop shooting! Who's there?" a voice called out, then repeated the question in Spanish.

"That's Christine," Kinley whispered.

"Are you sure?"

She nodded.

"Call out," he said.

"Christine?" she shouted. "Dr. Banks?"

"Kin…Kinley? Is that you?"

"Yes! It's me!" She tried to push up, but he held her down. He didn't want someone taking another shot at her.

"Oh my god! What are you doing here? I thought…never mind. Come down!"

Kinley looked at him with wide, questioning eyes.

"I have a bad feeling about this," he said in a low voice.

"What else are we going to do?"

He could evade without her, but there was no way he would risk it with her. "Hang on." He pulled out the satellite phone he'd shoved in his pocket before they left the campsite, leaving everything else there with the intention of returning. Sending their position to the team in Flores, he zeroed the device, deleting all the information on it, and shoved it into a tangle of brush next to them.

"Okay. Stay behind me." Standing up, he held his hands in the air and picked his way to the edge of the clearing.

An older blond woman stood between two men. "No. No need for that. Come on." She said something to the two men with guns. They lowered them and slung them over their shoulders and walked back toward the tents.

She waved at Shane and Kinley to join her.

He still had a bad feeling in his gut—something was off.

Once they cleared the edge of the jungle, Christine jogged to Kinley, pulling her into a hug. "I've been so worried about you. The driver came back and said you weren't at the hotel and your room had been ransacked."

"Someone attacked me and I had to run," Kinley said.

Christine gasped and held Kinley away from her by the shoulders, scanning her from head to toe. "What? Are you all right?

What happened? How did you get here?"

"We hiked," Kinley said. "Through the jungle for the past three days."

She looked between Kinley and Shane. "Oh, my dear. You poor thing. Did the man who attacked you get your notebook?"

Shane saw the moment it clicked with Kinley. How did Christine know Kinley had been attacked by one man and that he'd been after her notebook?

Kinley eased away from Christine and closer to Shane. "No. But—I don't understand. How did you know they wanted my notebook? Why were you with those men?"

She looked between them. "What men?"

"In the black SUVs—at the hotel the night I was attacked. A man shoved you against the car. The same man who tried to give me a ride to Carmelita. I thought they had kidnapped you."

Christine's entire demeanor changed. Until that moment, Shane would have said she was an attractive older woman, but a hardness entered her face, emphasizing the pinched quality of her lips and eyes.

"Well, I wish I had known that before. I would have played up that angle."

"What?" Kinley asked.

"I wasn't kidnapped, silly girl. That was a lovers' quarrel. We hit a wall with the translations. I wanted to wait for the driver to pick you up like we planned, but after three months in this godforsaken jungle Armando was impatient."

Kinley shook her head. "I don't understand. Where is Dr. Biert and the rest of the team?"

Christine rolled her entire head. "Ugh. There's no team. It's just us."

"But the emails. The invitation from the Foundation…"

"Dummy accounts. Fake. I knew you needed a little incentive. You wouldn't have come if you knew it was a private endeavor. You're too invested in the peer review process.

"Don't get me wrong, the Foundation plans on uncovering the city—eventually—but with a different team. They had the audacity to give the lead to someone else. To a man, of course. I've worked my entire life for this moment and they were going to hand it to someone less experienced simply because he has a dick between his legs. It's bullshit.

"Armando agreed to fund my project for eighty percent of whatever we discover. It's priceless and I can live comfortably on twenty percent of priceless, so what do I care?"

She shrugged and turned to the camp. "Come along."

He was no psychologist, but that woman was batshit crazy.

"What do I have to do with this?" Kinley asked when they reached the tents.

"My dear girl. When you sent me that email telling me you deciphered the Lago Azul text, I couldn't believe it. It was like Kinich Ahau himself was smiling down on me. The inscriptions in the temple are the exact same as the text. You, my dear, are the key to finding the treasure of Aapo."

"That's…that's a myth." Kinley glanced at Shane. He wanted to find a way to reassure her but couldn't figure out the best way to do it.

Christine leaned close. "But it's not. We found the burial chamber. And you're going to figure out how to open it."

Kinley's mind jumped from one thing to the other as they followed Christine toward the temple. She searched blindly for Shane's hand and some of her fear disappeared once hers was engulfed in his, along with a reassuring squeeze. He wouldn't let anything happen to her.

Christine and her team had cleared patches along the base until they'd found an entrance. Much of the facade was still covered with plants and trees staking their claim in whatever small crevice they could find.

One thing bothered her more than anything else she'd learned in the last ten minutes. "Why did you have us attacked on the road from Flores if you intended on sending a driver for me?"

Christine stopped and faced them, a look of derision marring her complexion. "What are you talking about?"

"The tour van we took from the airport—it was attacked by bandits on the way to Carmelita. Our driver was shot and almost killed," she said.

"We had nothing to do with that," Christine said.

"Really? Because he was one of the ones who attacked us." Shane pointed at one of the men ahead of them on the path. "How's the head?"

The man snarled and took a menacing step forward. Kinley startled and edged closer to Shane.

Christine stopped him with a raised hand. "Is that true?"

"*El Capitán's* orders. He wanted the notebook without the difficulty of the girl."

Christine's eyes narrowed and she pursed her lips.

"Let's go." She spun on her heel and marched toward the temple entrance.

Kinley looked at Shane. He winked at her. Winked! She gaped at him.

Pulling her close, he put his mouth to her temple. "Easiest way to get the upper hand when you're outgunned and outnumbered is to sow discord and discontent."

What? Upper hand of what? Of who? More importantly, what was he planning?

"Let's go!" Christine shouted from the entrance.

"*Vámonos*." The man behind them pushed her between the shoulders. Shane resisted and tried to turn to face him.

"No," she said under her breath. "Come on."

Shane went reluctantly, but herded Kinley ahead of him and placed himself between her and the guy.

"Not you." Christine pointed at the two guards. "Go back to the camp."

The men exchanged glances before shrugging and leaving them.

"Dickheads," she muttered. "Follow me."

Kinley ducked her head to follow Christine through the entrance. Glancing behind her, she saw Shane hunched at the waist, his wide shoulders brushing the sides of the tunnel as they walked.

"You okay?" she asked.

"Dandy."

She smiled at his surly tone. In any other situation it would be hilarious. With her mentor losing her mind and men pointing guns at them, it was only mildly amusing.

Whoever was funding the operation had run lights through the tunnel and the dim glow cast deep shadows on the walls. After a few yards, they entered a small chamber about ten feet square. Tunnels led in each direction and Christine turned left. At the next chamber, she continued straight and ascended steep, rough-hewn steps.

Kinley didn't think to count the steps until they'd already climbed a dozen or so. Numbers were important to the Mayans and she knew the number of steps would be significant. In the chamber at the top of the steps, Christine turned right, then straight through the next chamber followed by a right, left down some steps, then left and down again until their path dead-ended in a chamber much larger than any of the others they'd passed through.

"Oh my god," Kinley whispered in awe.

"Gods," Christine said. "This is the chamber of the gods. At least that's what I'm calling it."

"I don't give a shit what you call it as long as she can figure out where the fucking tomb is."

Kinley gasped and spun toward the center of the chamber. Shane shuffled her to the side and stepped in front of her. A man rose from the altar and she flinched back. The same man who'd offered her a ride at the airport in Flores. It was all starting to make twisted sense.

Disappointment, shame, and a host of other ugly emotions swirled in her stomach with the sharp bite of acid. All this time, she'd trusted Christine. Confided in her. Shared her discovery with her and then had been betrayed by her.

"Who is he?" The man pointed at Shane.

"My boyfriend." Kinley stepped from behind Shane and took his hand. If they knew he was more than just an average Joe, they might hurt him. She wasn't too proud to admit she was out of her element and royally screwed if she had to fend for herself.

The man looked at Christine, who shrugged. "Whatever." He swung his legs over the side of the altar and kicked his heels against the stone. "We are going to set the charges today."

"I told you, we are not blowing up the walls. We can't make it look like there was never any treasure if there's a fucking hole blown in the wall," Christine said through clenched teeth.

The man must be Armando, who appeared unbothered by the fact he was lounging on a sacrificial altar. Kinley suppressed a shudder.

"Who cares if there is a hole in the wall? Or every wall?"

"I care. Because I still need to be able to write up the find and I can't exactly do that if it looks like I looted the damn place first."

"Again—who cares? We're going to be so damn rich you'll never have to beg for scraps from a bunch of intellectual rejects again. We'll blow it and be out of this fucking jungle before the end of tomorrow."

Christine pulled a handgun from the small of her back, pointed it at Armando, and shot him.

Kinley screamed and slapped her hands over her ears as the sound echoed off the stone walls.

"I am sick and tired of men telling me what I can and cannot do." Christine looked at her. "Figure out how to get into the tomb and we'll both make history."

All she could do was stare at the woman she'd admired and trusted for so long. What had happened to her?

Christine raised the gun and pointed it at Shane. "I just killed the man I've been fucking for almost two years. Don't think I'll hesitate to shoot your boyfriend to get you to cooperate."

Kinley spared a glance at the man sprawled on the altar, his blood creeping toward the channels that would drain it from the top.

"Okay," she whispered. Looking up at Shane, she held out her hand. "Can I have my notebook?"

"Kin." His eyes were trying to telegraph a message, but she didn't know what. All she knew was the best way to get them out of there was to solve the puzzle.

"It's okay," she assured him.

Shane pulled her notebook from his cargo pocket and handed it to her. She managed a tight smile and faced the wall closest to the entrance. It was time to actually analyze the carvings instead of just looking at them.

She could do this.

Christine might kill them as soon as she did, but maybe she could give Shane time to devise a plan. He'd snapped an armed man's neck—here was hoping he could disarm a woman having one hell of a midlife crisis.

CHAPTER 13

"Can we get some food in here?" Shane asked. He'd leaned against the wall closest to the chamber entrance.

"No," Christine said. She was pacing in front of the wall to his right, her gaze never leaving Kinley, who was working on the wall directly across from her, with the altar in between them.

"How about some water?" he asked.

"No."

"So your plan is to starve and dehydrate us. Got it."

Christine checked her watch. "We'll break for the day in two hours. You can eat and drink then."

Two hours, plus the hour or more they'd already spent there, should be plenty of time for Leonidas to send in the team. He regretted ditching the satellite phone, not that it would have worked under the tons of stone above their heads, but he felt naked and vulnerable without a way to communicate with them. He had some glint tape stashed on his clothes, but the only way to place it anywhere as a signal was to leave the pyramid and he wasn't about to leave Kinley alone with the crazy lady.

Christine had calmed down once Kinley started working and

kept her full attention on Kinley while she muttered and jotted notes in her notebook.

"How did you guys get in here? I didn't see a clearing large enough for a helicopter." Which meant the one they'd heard yesterday had been just a coincidence, unless it was dropping supplies to the camp.

"They bulldozed a road through the jungle and drove in."

Kinley turned around. "You bulldozed a road through the jungle?"

Shane thought that was a ballsy move as well.

"Not me," Christine said. "Them."

He noticed she did that a lot—blamed something on "them" instead of taking any responsibility for her involvement.

"Are the guards loyal to you or the dead guy?" He needed to know the level of threat they were going to face leaving the temple.

Christine diverted her attention away from Kinley to glare at him. "You ask a lot of questions."

Shane held up his hands in mock surrender. "Hey, I'm just worried about what they're going to do when we leave here and they find out their boss is dead."

She stared at him for several minutes. Had he taken the hapless boyfriend act a bit too far?

"They're loyal to getting paid. Now shut up." She returned to watching Kinley.

He waited and watched. Just when her shoulders began to relax, he asked, "When was the last time they got paid?"

"I swear to—"

"They're prayers," Kinley interrupted. "They're all prayers. This isn't a tomb, it's a sacrificial chamber—that's it."

"Bullshit." Christine sneered. "We are in the precise center of the pyramid. This is where all the important tombs were found in the existing pyramids and this is where Aapo's tomb is, so find it."

"It's not here! Look." Kinley turned back to the wall behind her. "God of maize." She pointed to the large medallion in front of her then stepped to her right. "Goddess of birth and fertility. God of rain. God of sun. Goddess of family. God of life."

She pointed at the large, gold-covered medallion in the center of the wall directly across from him. "God of death...and the afterlife..."

"What? What is it?" Christine asked.

Shane joined Kinley in front of the wall. She didn't say anything but went around the room and scanned the medallions, one hand tracing each one without touching it, while she mumbled to herself.

"What is it?" Christine asked loudly.

Kinley's head whipped around, her ponytail swinging with her. "That medallion is upside down."

"Is that important?" Shane asked.

"Maybe." She returned to stand in front of the medallion in question. "This symbol here"—she pointed to the bottom of the circle—"is at the top of all the other medallions."

Christine pressed her face against the wall next to the stone circle. "There's a gap. It looks like it's attached to the wall instead of carved from it." She stepped back and looked at Shane. "Turn it."

"Uh. I've seen this movie. I turn the big Mayan wheel of death and the afterlife and poison darts shoot from the walls, the floor drops out, the ceiling collapses, and we all die. No thanks."

"That only happens in movies," Kinley said. "There has never been a tomb found with booby traps."

Shane crossed his arms. "Don't care."

Christine took a more hardline approach to convincing him. Taking a step away from the wall, she pointed the gun at Kinley. "Turn the wheel."

Kinley stared at him with wide, frightened eyes. Fuck. He didn't have a good feeling about this. Not that he thought the ceiling would actually collapse or a giant boulder would roll on top of them, but he had no doubt Christine would kill them both the moment they outlived their usefulness.

"Step to the side," he told Kinley. Wiping his hands on his pants, he grasped the edges of the medallion. The gap was too small to fit his fingers in, so he gripped it like a rock climber and hoped the Mayans adhered to lefty-loosey.

He strained against the wheel for almost a minute. Just as he made the decision to try the other direction, it shifted a hair with a fall of dust. He snatched his hands from the stone and looked at Kinley.

"It moved," she said. Her green eyes shone with excitement and he grinned.

"Keep going," Christine said behind them.

For a moment, he'd forgotten they weren't alone. Judging by the way Kinley's joy dissipated, so had she. Gripping the stone, he tried to get it to turn again, succeeding in getting another inch before having to take a break. Over the pounding of his heart, he heard three short taps.

"What was that?" Christine asked.

"What?" Kinley asked.

"That noise." She looked around the chamber.

"I didn't hear anything," Kinley said.

"I heard tapping."

"Maybe whatever mechanism this is attached to runs through the chamber and it settled?" She shrugged.

He didn't know whether she honestly hadn't heard the signal or if she was trying to distract Christine. "Maybe it's the poison darts cocking into position."

"Shut up and keep turning," Christine moved away from the back wall.

Perfect. Shane smirked at her and looked at Kinley. "Ready?"

She inhaled and blew out a breath. "Ready."

Placing his hands back on the stone, he widened his stance and licked his lips. This was going to suck if he was wrong.

"Now!"

He grabbed Kinley and engulfed her in his arms, taking her to the floor as the lights went out, plunging them into complete darkness. A shot rang out and sparks ricocheted off the wall exactly where Kinley had been standing.

"Get down!"

"Drop the gun!"

"Shane? You good?"

"We're good," he said. "You're good, right?" he asked against Kinley's hair.

"You're squishing my boob," she said.

"Oh, shit. Sorry." He relaxed his hold.

"Tango secured. Shane, if you're done playing nookie, we're bringing the lights back on."

"Fuck off, Devon," Shane said.

Devon laughed and counted down from three. Shane closed his eyes, then blinked them open to let them readjust from the total darkness. Visually checking that Kinley was unharmed, he gripped the side of her face and kissed her. Fuck, he'd been so afraid she'd be hurt during the takedown, he hadn't even been able to contemplate it beforehand. Now his whole body shook with relief.

He pressed his forehead against hers. "You're okay."

"I'm okay," she whispered.

"Y'all going to stay down there all night?"

Shane looked over his shoulder to find Harrison standing over them in full kit.

"Yeah," Shane said. "Do you mind?"

Kinley slapped his shoulder. "No. Let me up."

He sighed and rolled to his feet, then helped her stand.

Christine sat near the altar, her hands bound behind her back, tears streaming down her face and a look of unadulterated rage directed at them. Devon and Jordan stood next to her.

"Kinley, this is Devon, Harrison, and Jordan. They're part of

Leonidas. Guys, this is Kinley." They all waved and said hello while Shane ran his hand down her shoulder and arm one more time. He needed the contact.

"Let's get out of here," he said.

"Wait." She looked at the medallion, then back at him.

"You want to open it?"

She licked her lips and nodded.

He glanced at his teammates, who all shrugged. Except Harrison, who raised his gun to the low-ready.

"What are you doing?" Shane asked.

Harrison looked at him like he was crazy. "Mummies, man."

Shane looked at Kinley and raised an eyebrow. "See?"

She rolled her eyes and gestured to the medallion.

He chuckled and gripped the edges, straining to turn the wheel. He managed an impressive twenty degrees or so before his strength gave out.

"Here. Switch out," Devon said. He swung his rifle behind his back and took Shane's place. He managed another few inches before switching out with Jordan. Harrison stayed in the background, ready to shoot any cursed undead that popped out.

Little by little they turned the wheel until it was upright and settled into something with a deep thunk. They stepped back and glanced around the room.

Waiting.

For…nothing. Nothing happened.

"Now what?" Devon asked.

"I don't know," Kinley said. "I mean, the temple has been here for thousands of years. Whatever was supposed to do…whatever…could be stuck, it could be deteriorated, or…" She shrugged.

"Or?" Shane asked.

"Or there's nothing to find and the medallion was just upside down."

"What if we push on the wall?" Harrison asked.

"Not worried about mummies now?" Jordan asked.

"Oh, I'm still worried, but I'm invested now. I want to know what's behind the wall."

"Kinley?" Shane asked.

She shrugged again. "Sure."

Shane's teammates joined him along the wall, two on either side of the medallion, and braced their shoulders. "One… two…three!"

He grunted as he put his weight against the wall, his feet sliding on centuries of dust on the floor. He wanted the damn thing to move. He didn't want to see the disappointment in Kinley's eyes again.

The wall lurched a foot and they stumbled upright, looking at each other in astonishment.

"Holy shit," Harrison said.

"Keep pushing?" Devon asked.

"Hang on." Kinley peered at the edge of the wall. "Does anyone have a flashlight?"

"Here." Jordan held out a small black light.

She clicked it on and shined it along the edge of the wall on either side. "There's a void. I think the wall will slide in."

They found handholds and pushed the wall in the direction she indicated. Inch by inch another room was revealed. They stopped when the heavy stone panel was half of the way in the recess, opening a space wide enough for three of them to stand shoulder to shoulder. Without discussing it, they stepped back and let Kinley shine the light inside.

"Oh. My. God. It's real."

"Ho-lee shit," Harrison said.

Jordan leaned his arm against Shane's shoulder. "That's gold, right?"

"It's mine! I found it!" Christine pointed the gun she held right at Kinley.

"No!" Shane dove for Kinley, knocking her to the ground.

Shots rang out and fire burst to life in his back.

"Shane. Shane!"

CHAPTER 14

"No. Nonononono." Kinley struggled under the weight of Shane's body. Over his shoulder, she could see the blood spreading across his back. "Shane. Shane! Help him!"

Two of the men lifted Shane off her while the other one helped her upright. She jerked her arm from his grasp and crawled to Shane. "Please don't be dead."

"He's not, but you need to let us work on him," one of them said. Jordan, maybe? She couldn't remember their names. She should, but she couldn't. Not right now.

She spared a glance at Christine lying at the base of the altar, her eyes wide and unseeing, a dark crimson flower blooming on her chest. "How did she get the gun?"

"It was still on the floor," Jordan said. "It was kicked out of the way when we took her down. None of us bothered to pick it up since she was secure. How'd she get her arms in front of her?"

"Yoga," Kinley said. "She did yoga religiously."

"Fuck," one of the guys next to Shane said. "We need to get him topside. I can't get Turner on the radio under all this stone."

One of them handed his gun to Jordan and hefted Shane onto his shoulder. She clapped her hands over her mouth when he jostled Shane into a better position. God, he was so big. She'd laughed when he'd been hunched over in the entry tunnel, but they were all going to hunch—how were they going to get him out of there?

"Kinley, can you lead the way?" Jordan asked. "I'll be right behind you."

"What?" She looked from Shane to him. "Yes. I think so." All she had to do was follow the lights, right?

Leading the way out of the chamber, she spared one last glance for Christine. She should feel something—regret, hate, *something*. All she felt was numb. She started off slowly, worried the team wouldn't be able to keep up with their gear and carrying Shane, until one of them asked if she could go faster. She could sprint for the exit if they needed to, but she settled on a jog. The rattle of their gear echoed behind her.

What was that doing to Shane's injuries? Was it making them worse? They hadn't even sealed the bullet holes like Oakley had done with Jorge's wound. Did that mean Shane was better or worse? Was he already dead and they weren't telling her?

The final set of steps appeared and she angled her body through the last tunnel. She turned to watch the team exit, walking backward to give them space until she tripped over a stump, landing hard on her ass and back. Pushing up, she scrambled backward. She hadn't tripped over a stump, but over the body of one of the guards.

Jordan helped her up once again. "Sorry. Should have warned you we cleared the camp."

"It's okay. Probably not something you usually have to tell people."

He shrugged like it was something that happened more frequently than she thought. She opened her mouth to ask exactly how often but stopped at the sight of Devon and Harrison—their names finally coming back to her—exiting the tunnel, carrying

Shane between them. They laid him on the ground right away and knelt beside him.

"Helo's three minutes out," Jordan said.

Kinley grasped her hands tight under her chin. She'd never, ever been the hand-wringing type, but the sight of Shane flat on the ground while his teammates attended to him was more than she could bear.

"Hey." Jordan touched her shoulder. "We've got him. We won't let him go without a fight."

She closed her eyes, tears tracking down her cheeks, and nodded, grateful he wasn't feeding her a crap load of platitudes about everything being fine.

"Kinley, how are you with heights?" Jordan asked.

Her brows pinched together. "Okay, I guess. Why?"

"The helicopter can't land here, so we're going to have to hoist up."

"What does that mean?"

"The engineer is going to drop a cable, we're going to hook into it, and they're going to pull us up."

Kinley's eyebrows rose while she opened and closed her mouth. "Oh. Uh…okay. What about Shane?"

"They're going to do the same with him," he said.

"His wounds—"

"They know what they're doing, Kinley."

She swallowed hard while her heart *whomped, whomped* in her chest. Shane was so pale. They'd cut his shirt off and had his chest wrapped in wide green and white bandages. Blood was already seeping through. There was no other choice but to trust them.

The wind whipped up and grew more and more forceful. The *whomp, whomp* wasn't her heart, but the rotor blades of the black helicopter hovering over them.

"Come over here," Jordan shouted. He led her out from under the belly of the helicopter and pulled her down to a kneeling position, tucking her head down and covering most of her body with his.

The wash from the blades whipped her clothes and hair around her, throwing up leaves and sticks.

"Keep a hand over your eyes," he shouted near her ear. "Keep your eyes on the ground, I'll lead you over and hook you up. Okay?"

"Okay!"

He took her upper arm and led her back toward the group. She curved a hand over her eyes to protect them and kept her head bent when he stopped.

"Raise your arms," he shouted.

She did as he asked and he slipped a wide, thick canvas loop under her arms.

"Hold on here." He took her hands and placed them on the canvas, almost in front of her face. He shimmied into a second loop, then raised and lowered one arm.

"Hang on!"

A sharp squeak escaped when the cable drew taut and her feet left the ground. She squeezed her eyes closed. Maybe she hadn't given enough thought to whether or not she had an issue with heights. Of course, she hadn't had all the information when he'd asked that question. Had he asked whether she had an issue with being dragged up in the air on a cable and a loop, she might have answered differently. The force of the wind from the blades whipped her hair around her head and face, lashing the skin around her eyes and mouth with the ends.

They stopped moving and she felt Jordan lean close again. "Lift your feet. The engineer is going to grab you and pull you back."

Sure enough, as soon as she lifted her feet in front of her, hands grasped the material at her hips and pulled her back until she hit the rough floor of the helicopter with a jolt. She blinked her eyes open. Jordan's feet were braced on the edge of the opening while he held on to a bar over his head. The man next to her lifted the loop over her head and handed her a set of large headphones attached to a cord. He gestured for her to put them on and she slipped them over her ears. They immediately muted the noise from the helicopter.

"Move back," he said.

Kinley glanced behind her and scooted back on her butt, using her feet to propel across the floor. He helped her into a seat and snapped the harness around her.

Jordan hooked a cord from his belt to a ring on the inside ceiling of the helicopter and slipped from the loop. Then he leaned out of the helicopter.

She gasped, expecting him to fall, but the cord kept him in place. Another cry escaped when she saw the top of Shane's head appear. Jordan leaned down and helped haul him into the helicopter. Devon and Harrison appeared quickly.

"We're in," one of the men said. His voice sounded hollow coming through the earphones.

The group unhooked from the cable and snapped their cords to rings in the floor. Jordan and the man who helped her in moved the metal arm that held the winch into the helicopter and slammed the sliding door shut.

"All secure."

"We're out," came the reply.

Helpless, Kinley watched while they inserted an IV line into Shane's arm. His eyes fluttered and his lips moved, but she couldn't hear what he said. One of the men leaned his ear close to Shane's mouth, then looked at Kinley before replying to him. Whatever he said didn't come over her headset, but Shane struggled to angle his head in her direction and he lifted his free hand.

Her heart lurched in her chest and she jerked against the harness. Glancing down, she pulled and pushed, but couldn't figure out how to release the belts. The man who'd buckled it leaned over Shane and twisted the center of the circle, releasing all the buckles at once.

Throwing her headset aside, she fell to her knees at Shane's head and grasped the side of his face in her palm. Pressing her lips to his temple, she said, "I'm here. I'm here. Stay with me, Shane. You have to stay with me."

"Found you," he mumbled. His eyes fluttered closed and she snapped her gaze to Jordan, kneeling on the other side of him.

He mouthed, "Passed out."

Looking at Shane again, she pressed her fingers to the pulse in his throat, finding the strong, but slow pulse.

"I'm here," she whispered against his forehead.

The ride was shorter than she expected and yet the longest seventy-six minutes of her life. As soon as they touched down, Devon threw open the door. Devon and Jordan jumped down, leaving their guns tucked behind some green netting in the back of the helicopter.

Through the open door, Kinley saw four people in scrubs jogging toward them, the two in the rear pulling a gurney between them. From her vantage point, she could see the tops of other buildings around them. When they reached the side of the helicopter, they transferred Shane to the gurney with Devon and Jordan's help, then raced back the way they came. She tried to scramble out of the helicopter—if she didn't hurry, they'd get in the elevator without her and then she'd lose them, but Devon and Jordan climbed back in and stopped her.

"Let me out!"

Jordan grabbed her around the waist when she tried to squeeze between them. The door slid shut and they lifted off,

"No! Take me back!"

"Calm down, Kinley. You'll be back, but we have to get you somewhere safe first."

She pressed a hand against the window, watching the building grow smaller and smaller the farther away they flew. There wasn't anywhere safer than with Shane—didn't they know that?

Less than ten minutes later, they landed again and the pilot cut the engine before they opened the door. This time, two men and a woman waited on the edge of the small concrete pad.

Jordan helped her down from the helicopter and led her toward the small group.

"Miss Dunn?" the woman asked.

"Yes," she said.

"Belinda Parker. Welcome to the U.S. Embassy."

CHAPTER 15

Shane flinched and swatted at whatever was trying to crawl up his nose. Pain shot across his shoulder and back and he groaned.

"Oh, good. You're awake."

He blinked his dry and gritty eyes several times and tried to focus on Paige.

"Did you stick something up my nose?" He rubbed the underside—slowly this time.

"Maybe. You were taking too long to wake up."

He glanced around the hospital room. "Where are we?"

"Charleston. You were transferred here after they stabilized you in Guatemala."

"I feel like someone took a sledgehammer to my back." He flexed his shoulders to test the amount of pain and regretted it immediately.

"The bullet traveled under your shoulder blade and they had to dig it out. That should have been the end of it but, being your difficult self, you developed a fever, so they kept you under while they tried to get it down."

Closing his eyes, he nodded. "How did Christine get the gun? Her hands were behind her back."

"Yoga, I think," Paige said.

He opened his eyes and squinted at her. "What?"

"Kinley said she did yoga. I figure she was able to slip her hands under her ass then slipped her legs through her arms. I haven't been able to do that since I was nine."

"You found yourself tied up a lot as a kid?"

"My brother was a shit when we were growing up."

The corners of his mouth turned up briefly. "Is she dead?"

She nodded. He nodded back and closed his eyes again. He was seriously tired, but he had more questions.

"Where's Kinley?"

Paige brushed at the edge of her skirt. "As far as I know, she's back in North Carolina."

"What do you mean, as far as you know?"

"When we evacuated you out, she was transferred to the U.S. Embassy in Guatemala City. From there, she was sent to D.C. to answer questions from the Guatemalan government. We felt it was better for her to be back on U.S. soil before answering any questions about bodies and priceless treasure."

"Jesus," he said. "You had her do that on her own?"

She scoffed. "Of course not. We sent Jocelyn Gantry to act as her lawyer."

That was something at least. He would have rather been there with her, but that obviously wasn't possible.

"Right. On to business," Paige said. "This has been an expensive vacation for Leonidas. Thankfully, the International Archaeological Foundation and the Government of Guatemala have contracted with us for site security of the excavation of the ruins."

That got his attention. "Who's leading the dig? From the Foundation?"

"I'd have to look it up, but I think it's a Dr. Bright or Bart. Something like that."

"Biert?" he asked.

She nodded. "That might be it."

"That's bullshit. Kinley should be the lead on the dig—she found it! It was her research that led to the discovery. She deserves the credit!"

"You need to calm down before you pull something," Paige said. "I don't know how the decision was made or who else is on the team. All I know is he is the person we were given as the point of contact for coordination. You might also be interested to know that both you and Kinley are receiving a quarter of a percent finder's fee."

"A whole quarter of a percent, huh?" Not that he wasn't interested, but he doubted that would be any consolation to Kinley. She wanted to be part of the discovery. She wanted the credit, not the riches—not that a quarter of a percent sounded like a lot anyway.

"The overall worth of the treasure that's been found *so far* is estimated to be around half a billion dollars."

His jaw dropped.

"Yeah. Congratulations. You're a millionaire and everyone gets bonuses this year. Except you. As soon as you're well enough, you'll take over as security site lead." She cocked her head. "Unless you'd prefer to do something else and not return to Guatemala."

Shane was still gaping at her when she dropped that second bomb. "No. I want the site lead." If there was any chance at all of Kinley returning to the site, he wanted to be there. And if she wasn't invited, he'd make damn sure she was.

"Good. I'll leave you to rest."

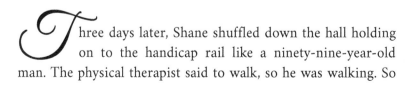

Three days later, Shane shuffled down the hall holding on to the handicap rail like a ninety-nine-year-old man. The physical therapist said to walk, so he was walking. So much, the nurses yelled at him after his third lap around the hall.

This weakness was bullshit. He needed to be better. Today. He had shit to do. At the top of his list—trying to call Kinley again. Paige had sent his phone and clothes from the camp site in Guatemala and he'd called Kinley's number as soon as it had charged. Unfortunately, it had gone directly to voice mail every time and he didn't know if she'd gotten hers back. Her mailbox was full, so he couldn't even leave a message.

He reached his room and eased onto the bed, shifting and grunting his way onto his back. Centered in the bed, he released all the tension in his muscles. Fuck. He hated taking painkillers, but he might have reached his threshold for the day.

A soft knock drew his attention. Kinley stood in the doorway, a shy, unsure smile on her lips. He'd never been so fucking happy to see anyone in his entire life.

"Can I come in?" she asked.

The pain forgotten, he eased up on his elbows. "God, yes. Come here." He held out his right arm since it didn't hurt as much when he moved it.

As soon as she was within reach, he pulled her close and pressed his lips to hers. She tasted like rich coffee, sweet caramel, and forever.

He loved her. Not just thought he did but knew it in the marrow of his bones. But he didn't want to tell her there, laid up in a hospital without being able to get down on his knees and beg her to let him find a way to make it work. He'd quit Leonidas, if that was what it took. He didn't care if he had to carry all her tools for the next sixty years while she deciphered ancient writing all over the world, as long as they were together.

She pulled away too soon. "I'm hurting you."

"No, you're not." Falling back on the bed didn't help his argument.

"Shane. I can feel you grimacing against my lips."

"Maybe a little, but it was totally worth it." He ran his fingers through the soft waves of her hair, hanging loose around her shoulders. "You're here."

"I'm here." She smiled and eased away, sitting on the edge of the bed when he refused to let go of her hand.

"Paige told me about Christine. Are you okay?"

She nodded and took a shaky breath. "I'll get there. I'm having a hard time understanding what drove her to that point. I mean, I get being ambitious and being discounted as a woman, but not to the point where people die because of it." She shook her head. "But mostly—I miss her. I miss the woman I *knew* and I feel bad about that."

"Don't." He tucked a strand of hair behind her ear. "Celebrate that woman. She had to have had some really good qualities at one time to have earned your respect and trust. Miss *that* woman."

She offered him a tremulous smile. "How'd you get to be so smart?"

"I met this woman a couple weeks ago. Smartest person I know."

Laughing softly, she took a tissue from the box beside the bed and wiped her nose.

"How did you know I was here?" he asked.

"Paige. I had to go to Leonidas to prepare to return to Guatemala and I asked about you. She told me where to find you."

A lightness spread through his chest as if a too-heavy barbell had suddenly been lifted off his sternum. "You're going back to Guatemala?"

"Yes. The Foundation asked me to be on the team leading the excavation of the ruins."

"That's great! Congratulations." He kissed her knuckles.

"I accepted because I was told you were the lead for the security team."

"That's what I hear. As soon as I can do more than shuffle down the hall a few times."

"And you're okay with that?" She wouldn't look at him and picked at the edge of the sheet next to her leg.

His brows pinched together. "Yes. Of course, I'm okay with that. Why wouldn't I be?"

"It's a pretty long commitment."

He smoothed the worry lines between her eyebrows. "I'm okay with that."

"A few years long."

"Kin—I'm okay with that."

She finally smiled, then pulled her lower lip between her teeth and looked at him. "Me too."

"Good. Because you're stuck with me for a while."

"I am?"

"Yeah, you are."

Kinley leaned forward and pressed her lips to his. "I'm okay with that."

CHAPTER 16

"Ms. Dunn?"

Kinley looked up from the carving she was examining. "Kinley. You can call me Kinley." She was never going to get used to the deference these grad students showed her. She wasn't that much older than them.

The guy blushed. "Right. Uh, you wanted to know when they arrived. They just drove through the checkpoint."

Kinley grinned and jumped up from the short stool she sat on. "Thanks!" She dashed through the tunnels and chambers, having to backtrack twice when she turned the wrong way. Bursting from the entrance, she ran across the space between the temple and the new campsite.

Two weeks. She hadn't seen Shane in two weeks. Twice as long as the length of time she'd spent with him in Guatemala. It was honestly ridiculous. If any of her friends told her they'd fallen in love with a guy after only a few weeks, she'd tell them they were crazy. Especially when they'd been separated for most of that time. Angie, Leonidas's IT specialist, hadn't been able to get the network operating until five days ago, so they hadn't even been able to video chat more than a few times.

A large black SUV came down the lane they'd cleared to ensure no ruins were destroyed. It stopped at the edge of the camp and Shane exited the passenger side. He closed the door and scanned the camp. Eduardo, one of the drivers, pointed in Kinley's direction and Shane turned, breaking into a huge grin when he saw her running toward him.

At the last second prior to throwing herself at him, she remembered he was still recovering from being shot.

It didn't stop him though. As soon as she was in front of him, he grabbed her around the waist and hauled her up against him, his mouth devouring hers.

Kinley wrapped her arms around his neck and lost herself in the kiss. It was like being home after a long absence—familiar and safe, but exciting to find out what had changed since she'd been gone.

"Ivers, put her down before you pull something and end up back in the hospital. I can't afford to be here for another week."

Shane broke their kiss. "Shit," he muttered.

Kinley smiled and touched her forehead to his.

He put her down and loosened his hold around her waist. "Graham."

The tall man approached and held out his hand, forcing Shane to let go of her. Aiden Graham had taken some getting used to. His gruff, no-nonsense, do-it-my-way-so-it's-done-right attitude had made her nervous at first, but he was amusing when he wasn't in work mode and he'd gone to bat for her on more than one occasion with the Foundation.

"Good to see you, boss," Shane said.

"You too. I know you guys have some catching up to do, but I have a flight in a few hours and I need to bring you up to speed."

Shane glanced at Kinley and looked as disappointed as she felt. Standing on her toes, she kissed him on the cheek. "Go. Work comes first. Eduardo can take your bags to our tent."

He leaned close. "*Our* tent?"

Kinley glanced at Graham and blushed when she realized there were two other people she didn't recognize who had gotten out of the back of the SUV.

Shane smirked and kissed her quickly. "Students," he said. "Eduardo said you'd take care of them."

She sighed. As word had gotten out, they'd been getting half a dozen or so students every other day. These two would put them close to thirty. She needed to talk to Dr. Biert about putting up another dormitory tent.

"Okay," she said. "Do what you need to and I'll get them checked in. I'll see you later." It looked like her plan was going to be delayed.

She looked across the hood at the driver. "Eduardo, can you take Shane's bags to our tent?"

"*Sí, señorita.* I also have supplies for the cantina."

"Wonderful. *Gracias.*" She looked at Shane. "Welcome back."

He winked and walked off with Graham.

Her whole body sighed until she remembered the two new additions. Spinning around on her toes, she gave them her best *I am a serious academic and I did not just make a fool of myself in front of complete strangers* smile.

"Right. Welcome to *El Tesoro*. At least, that's what we're calling it until we find the actual name of the city. I'm Kinley Dunn." She shook each of their hands as they introduced themselves.

"Daniel."

"Brittany. Spelled like it's supposed to be spelled, not with an I." She blushed and looked down. "Sorry. I ramble when I'm nervous and I'm really excited to meet you, so I'm nervous and I'm rambling again."

Kinley pulled her lips between her teeth to keep from laughing. She remembered being in that position, awestruck that she was meeting one of her idols. Hard to believe she was now that person for someone. "It's all right. There's nothing to be nervous about. I'll take you to the administration tent and we'll get your bunk assignments and you can get settled in. You won't get your work assignments until the morning."

They grabbed their bags from the back of the SUV and followed her across the camp.

"Can I ask you something?" Daniel asked.

"Sure." Kinley braced, knowing what was coming since each new addition asked the same questions. It was almost comical at that point.

"Is it true Dr. Banks sacrificed her lover to try to open the hidden burial chamber?"

"No."

"But she did kill him?" Brittany asked.

"Yes, that part is true," Kinley said.

"Is it true you killed her?" Daniel asked.

It was always the men who asked that question. "No. She was killed when she tried to shoot me. Shane was shot protecting me."

"He's your boyfriend?" Brittany asked.

And it was always the women who asked that. "Yes, he's my boyfriend."

She heard Brittany's heartfelt sigh and smiled. *Right there with you.*

She dropped them off at check-in and stopped by the cataloguing tent next door. She pushed the tent flap aside and ducked in. It always felt like organized chaos in there. Each artifact they found was cleaned, photographed, catalogued, packed, and sealed in crates to be shipped on to the Ministry of Antiquities. The smaller pieces, anyway. Many of the pieces appeared to have been carved in place inside the temple and other buildings they'd uncovered so far.

"Dr. Biert?"

He looked up from the stone piece he'd been bent over. "Kinley, come look at this."

She smiled at the excitement in his voice. He was like that with every artifact they found.

Dr. Biert had been a revelation. She'd been less than thrilled when the Foundation had appointed him to oversee the excavation, but she hadn't had any say in the matter.

He'd apologized within minutes of arriving at camp and finding her. When she'd called him from the airport in Flores, he'd just gotten off the phone with his ex-wife. The divorce had been far from harmonious and he'd taken his anger out on her. He told her he didn't even realize what she'd been talking about until he saw it on the news.

He also claimed not to know about the emails or Christine's plans, even though she'd told Kinley he was one of the team leads.

Kinley had been cautious and understandably guarded at the beginning, but Dr. Biert had shown her nothing but respect and had consulted with her every step of the way, even though she was technically one of the least experienced members of the team. It hadn't hurt that Graham had run a background check on him and reassured her he was clean.

She let him ramble on about the significance of the piece, knowing he was wrapping up when he said, "It's marvelous. Simply marvelous."

"It is," she agreed.

"How are the translations going in the temple?" he asked.

"Much faster now that we've definitively established the bases. Do you have time after dinner tonight to go over some of the ones we did today?"

"Why don't we do it in the morning? I heard Shane arrived in camp not too long ago."

"Wow! Gossip spreads fast," she said.

Dr. Biert chuckled. "Eduardo stopped by to let me know he found some canned pears. But you two are like our own celebrity couple. I'm surprised you're here instead of catching up."

The way the inflection of his voice rose at the end let her know he meant sex when he said "catching up." She couldn't hold his gaze. It was almost as bad as if her father had asked why she wasn't getting laid.

Kinley cleared her throat. "He's with Graham going over the security since he has to leave this afternoon."

"Oh, that's right. Well, don't worry about tonight. We can go over all that in the morning," he said.

"Okay. After breakfast?"

"Perfect."

She said goodbye and stopped at one of the water tanks since she'd run off without her water bottle. A quick glance around the camp showed no sign of Shane or Graham. She checked her watch. Still at least two hours before Graham had to leave—she may as well head back to the temple.

~

Shane turned slowly and tried not to look like he was lost. Not lost exactly, but he couldn't remember which tent was his and Kinley's. He had it narrowed down to two but didn't want to be the dick that walked into the wrong one. First thing tomorrow he was numbering all the damn tents.

"Hey. Whatcha doin'?"

He spun at the sound of Kinley's voice as she stepped from between two of the tents.

"Uh." He had no good answer for that.

She raised her eyebrows. "Lost?"

"Not exactly," he said.

Pulling her lips between her teeth, she nodded. "Turned around?"

"More accurate."

Kinley chuckled and pointed to the third tent from the end. "That one."

It was the first of his two choices so he hadn't been too far off.

He let her lead the way, but as soon as they cleared the doorway, he swept her up in his arms and kissed her.

She groaned and opened for him, her tongue meeting his while her fingers gripped the back of his hair.

He laid her on the bed and followed her down, nestling his hips between her thighs.

"I missed you." Dragging his mouth along her jaw and neck, he slipped the buttons of her shirt through the holes, revealing the soft skin between her breasts.

She sighed and bowed her back. "I missed you too. I'm so happy you're back."

Shane pulled the tails of her shirt from the waist of her pants. "I'm not going anywhere anytime soon."

"Wait. Wait, wait." Kinley pushed against his shoulders and wriggled out from under him.

His heart thumped and froze in his chest. "What's wrong?"

"Nothing, but I want to show you something and if we get naked I'm not going to want to put clothes back on to show you." She buttoned her shirt and stood.

He flopped onto his back, both relieved and increasingly frustrated. "Now?"

Kinley scanned his body and he held out hope she'd change her mind and jump his bones, but she shook her head like she was freeing herself from a trance. "Yes. Now."

She patted his thigh and grabbed a large flashlight from the storage chest at the end of the bed. "Come on, we're losing the light."

Groaning, Shane rolled to standing and followed her out of the tent, taking her hand as she smiled up at him. Okay, that made his blue balls worth it.

Leading him across the clearing between the camp and temple, she surprised him by veering around the base of the temple. She glanced up at the setting sun and picked up her pace, forcing Shane to lengthen his stride.

On the far side of the temple, she walked a path that was still overgrown, but led to a smaller pyramid.

"Is this...?"

Glancing over her shoulder, she smiled and nodded.

A much simpler structure than the large pyramid, the steps ended in one large chamber at the top. Positioned in the center of the room was a gold sun, larger than the span of his arms, ablaze as it reflected the last rays of daylight.

"I'm calling it the house of the setting sun."

"Nice," he said. "And fitting."

The gold sun stopped shining as the sun dropped below the horizon.

Kinley clicked on the flashlight and shined it on the walls. "It's their story. The story of their lives. A blight overcame their crops and poisoned the water." She shined the light along the wall as she spoke. "Their children and elders began to die, so their chief consulted the gods. Sometime after there was a solar eclipse and he took that as a sign to follow the path of the rising sun. They abandoned their city and traveled east and the chief sacrificed himself to the gods to ensure the safety of his people."

"So he didn't kill all his people and bury himself with his treasure?" he asked.

She shook her head and wiped away the tears streaming down her face as she recounted the tale. Shane pulled her into his arms and pressed his lips to her temple. "The team must have been excited when you showed them this."

"I haven't yet." She tilted her head back. "I wanted you to be the first person I told. This is our story. This is what we came to find."

He tried to breathe past the lump in his throat. It meant more than he could voice that she waited for him to return to share her discovery. A discovery that would cement her standing in the archaeological community. The whole reason she had traveled to Guatemala in the first place.

He tucked a piece of hair behind her ear. "Butt-Ass Naked."

Her brows pinched together. "What?"

"That's what Ban stands for."

She grinned. "Why do they call you that?"

"We were drinking one night after we graduated BUD/S and I decided it would be a good idea to streak the base commander's house. Butt-ass naked."

Her head fell back as she laughed. "I get why you didn't want to tell me when we first met."

He brushed tears from her cheek. "I love you, Kinley Dunn. I want to always be the first person you share your discoveries with. I want you to be the one I always share my silly stories with.

"For the last few years I've felt lost. I only ever wanted to be a SEAL and when I couldn't be that anymore, I didn't know what to do with my life. I've been searching for something. I thought I came to Guatemala to find some adventure. Turns out all I needed to find was you."

She sobbed out a laugh. "I love you too. I promise to always be the adventure you need."

Their lips met, their kiss full of promises. He grasped the sides of her face and brushed a tear from her cheek.

"Does this mean we can go take our clothes off now?" he asked.

Kinley laughed and threw her arms around his neck. "Yes. Let's go get butt-ass naked."

ABOUT THE AUTHOR

Tarina is an award winning author who has spent her entire life in and around the military - first as a dependent and then as an enlisted Air Force member. She uses her life as inspiration for many of her stories, because truth is stranger (and funnier) than fiction.

Tarina is retired Air Force and a single mom of rambunctious twins. Her favorite hobbies are traveling and naps. You can find her trying to find the perfect writing spot with a cup of coffee next to her.

Stay Connected
Website
Email
Newsletter

ALSO BY TARINA DEATON

The Combat Hearts Series

Stitched Up Heart

Half-Broke Heart

Locked-Down Heart

Rescued Heart

Imperfect Heart

Holiday Heart (only available to newsletter subscribers)

The Jilted Duet

Make Me Believe

Believe In Me (Coming Soon)

The Leonidas Corporation

Found in the Lost

Truth in the Lie

Flaw in the Defense

Day in the Knight (coming soon)

CPSIA information can be obtained
at www.ICGtesting.com
Printed in the USA
BVHW071017030123
655447BV00012B/113